DEADBEAT

Extremities #1

Maxim Volk

SLASHIC HORROR PRESS

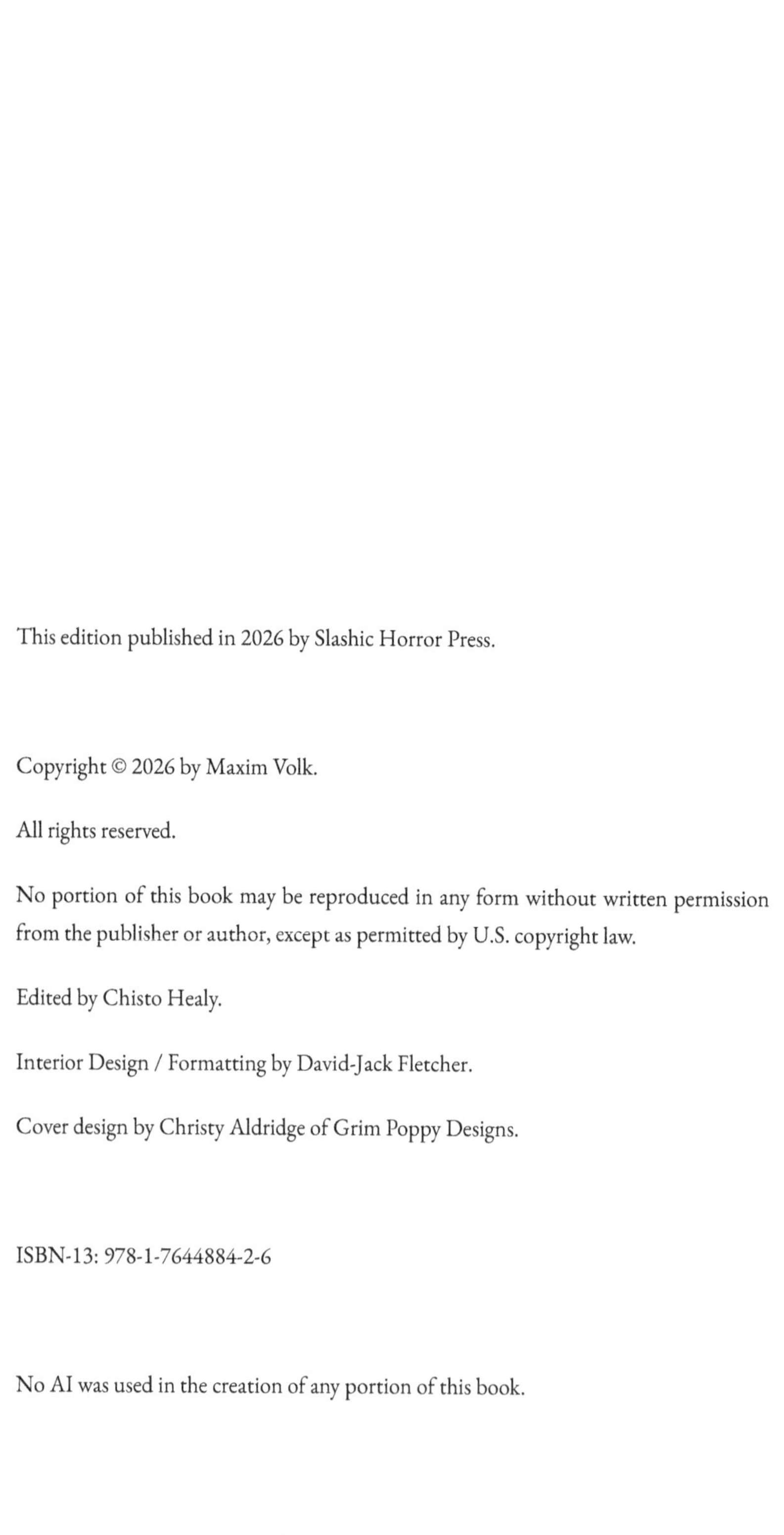

This edition published in 2026 by Slashic Horror Press.

Edited by Chisto Healy.

Interior Design / Formatting by David-Jack Fletcher.

Cover design by Christy Aldridge of Grim Poppy Designs.

ISBN-13: 978-1-7644884-2-6

No AI was used in the creation of any portion of this book.

START HERE

YOU ARE SITTING IN your bed, playing with your dick, looking at your husband Matt's suitcases in the bedroom that you share, trying not to be mad at him again for leaving for his business trip. He'll be gone two whole weeks, and in that time, he expects you to play the perfect househusband: cleaning, watching television, and working on that novel you've been swearing you're going to write but don't really even have an outline for. What he expects you not to do is get off with anyone. You're monogamous, despite his frequent travels, and the worst part? He doesn't even like getting off on video calls with you. Says he doesn't know when some creep might loop himself in and watch the pair of you jerking off manically at blurry glimpses of each other's nipples or cocks, as if that's something that happens. It's a ridiculous paranoia, as you keep telling him, but he insists on refraining from video sex, despite the length of his absence. It's going to be two long weeks of masturbating to whatever porn you can find on that social media app that has become overrun by Nazis. Even that shit is mostly AI now. Sometimes your husband pisses you off.

Matt enters the room. He is tall, dark, and handsome, and, dressed in his nice blue suit, he reminds you of that one hot evil business guy on that TV show set in the 60s. His jet-black hair is graying around the temples, and his eyes are kind and sparkling. He goes to the gym all the time, so his muscled frame strains against his suit. It's not the only thing. The crotch of his suit is too tight, and you can see the entire outline of his enormous member pressing against his body. "Hey, baby, the rideshare will be here soon." His voice is kind and gentle, like he's your dad telling his small child not to worry too much while he's gone. He's almost old enough to be your dad, but that's how you like it.

"I'm going to miss you," you say in your best baby voice, which, despite the frequency with which you pull it out of your repertoire, you know your husband does not find sexy. Usually, he'll scold you, saying you're too old for that, to which you'll respond that you're just his baby. This time, though, he's clearly thinking about something else.

"I'm going to miss you, too, hon," he says absently, leaning in to kiss you. You meet his lips with yours, puckering as you reach out to grab his dick. "Not now, baby; my ride is almost here."

You pout. "But I'm going to have two whole weeks where I won't be able to play with it. At least let me suck you off before you go."

He gives you a look of pity. "I can't be smelling like sex for my flight. Don't want to gross out my seatmates."

"Pweese." You feel debased even saying it, but you don't want to go two whole weeks without any action, especially considering the action has been a bit sparse as of late anyway.

"Sorry, baby. As soon as I get back. I promise." He grabs his suitcase and drags it down the stairs, each step making a ker-thunk noise. You hear the door shut downstairs, and you jump out of bed and watch as he walks towards his ride, his tight ass in those suit pants teasing you as he walks. Asshole. You flop back down on the bed.

As you sit, you fume, getting angrier and angrier. Fuck him. Fuck that loser and his business trips and his weird obsession with monogamy and his inability to get off over video call and his enormous dick that he wouldn't even let you suck off before he left you alone for two weeks, horny and bored with nothing to do. After enough fuming, and before he is even on the plane, you've decided you need to get off. You've cheated on him before, just as you're sure he's cheated on you on his business trips. You've seen the pictures that he's tagged in online during these trips, slutting it up at some bar in the 6-inch inseam pink shorts you picked out for him and the sparkly tank top he likes to wear when he's feeling sexy, something he should absolutely not be feeling a thousand miles away from you. In fact, he's probably eyeing some dude up at the airport right now. And what are you going to do about it? You're going to get off, too. Right now. Before he even lands in Detroit or Denver or wherever the fuck he's going, you're going to fuck some dude that you'll never see again. It's what Matt deserves for leaving you alone here.

Then again, it's risky. What if he forgot something and heads home now? You decide the risk is worth the reward. There are lots of ways that you could cheat on him. You could download that app you shouldn't have on your phone but have downloaded before. There's also your local sauna, a favorite gay cruising place of many a young gay man. Cheating would be a bit tacky, but he's left you alone for two weeks. What else are you going to do?

If you decide to download the cruising app you shouldn't have on your phone, go to page 17.

If you decide to hit up the local sauna, where you know dudes go for anonymous sex, go to page 7.

If you decide that cheating on your husband is tacky and/or gauche, go to page 5.

CHAPTER 1

YOU DECIDED THAT CHEATING ON YOUR HUSBAND IS TACKY AND/OR GAUCHE.

MAKE NO MISTAKE, MATT would absolutely deserve it if you cheated on him, and you are sure he's going to hook up with some hot little intern in the next two weeks, so really, you're taking the high road. You get a text from him on your phone. "Hey, baby, I'm boarding now, so I'm turning off my phone. I'll call you when I land. Love you!"

"Safe travels!" you type as you mutter obscenities about him leaving you horny at home. "Talk to you soon!"

You scroll through social media until you find a suitable porno: two nondescript muscle hunks jacking each other off. You prioritize speed over enjoying yourself, and you come in minutes. Then you set your phone down next to you and turn on the TV. The first thing you're greeted by is the weirdest advertisement you've ever seen. It starts with flashes of scenes from different zombie movies, some new, some old, and some that you don't recognize. Then a middle-aged man appears on screen. He is dressed like he is going on safari, in tan slacks, a tan button-down shirt, and a matching fedora that sits precariously on his head. He may have been cute once, but now he's pushing fifty, pasty, and a bit pudgy. He says, "Have you been plagued by the undead? Will one of your loved ones or hated ones just not stay deceased? I'm Rome Samuel, and I'm a certified zombie hunter. I make sure the dead stay dead. If you want someone back in the grave, give me a call." A number scrolls across the bottom of the screen. *It must be some kind of advertisement for a horror movie*, you think, *and a bad one at that*. You turn the TV off, disgusted by the weird commercial.

You're a bit sweaty, and a breeze is coming through the open window, giving you a chill. You walk over to the window and shut it. Still covered in jizz, you close your eyes for a quick nap. Unfortunately, with the window closed, there is no ventilation in the house. Your husband had reminded you a few times to change the batteries in the carbon monoxide detector, and eventually, to shut him up, you promised him you had changed them. The thing is, you're not very good at following through on promises or taking care of the house, despite that being the only thing you're supposed to be doing. As you doze, your house slowly fills with carbon monoxide. You drown in it in your sleep.

You are dead. Go to page 31.

CHAPTER 2

YOU DECIDE TO HIT UP YOUR LOCAL SAUNA.

YOU USED TO GO there all the time for anonymous sex before you met Matt, and this is not the first time you have gone there since your wedding. You've received some of the best orgasms of your life at that sauna, plus at least two cases of chlamydia. It's nearby too; you don't even need to drive. You pack a small bag with your shower shoes, a towel, a bottle of lube, and some condoms, and you head out.

The sauna is only a few blocks away. You stop at your local bodega for a bottle of sports drink to keep your electrolytes up for your impending sex adventure, nodding to Alexei, the burly Russian guy who works behind the counter, who asks, "This all, boss?" when you check out.

Leaving the bodega, you feel a buzz in your pocket and check your phone. You have a text from Matt. "Hey, baby, I'm boarding now, so I'm turning off my phone. I'll call you when I land. Love you!"

"Safe travels!" you type as you mutter obscenities about him leaving you horny at home and how he's forcing you to cheat on him. "Talk to you soon!"

It's only about five more minutes before you arrive at the sauna. You're greeted by a cute attendant with olive skin and a small mustache who is not wearing a shirt, a nice tease for what is to come. You pay the exorbitant one-time fee for entry, not feeling like a membership is necessary (though if you get what you came for, you may decide to get an ongoing membership for when your husband is out of town. It's his money anyway). Then, you make your way to the locker room to change.

In the locker room, you're greeted by a plethora of naked bodies, and you have to wait for a couple of minutes to change because you are already hard just from seeing the men of all shapes and sizes changing out of their clothes and into their birthday suits. There's a bulletin board on the wall, and you peruse it while you wait for your boner to go down. The bulletin board is full of random pieces of paper and business cards advertising local services, from carpet cleaners to realtors to escorts. One flyer catches your eye. This one is particularly weird. It is a mock-wanted poster with a picture of a zombie from an old movie. It reads, "Zombie Problems? Call Now," and then there's a number to call. At the bottom of the flyer, there is a smaller picture of a middle-aged, pasty white guy in a safari cosplay and a hideous chud fedora. Next to the photo is smaller text that reads "Rome Samuel, Zombie Hunter." What the fuck are people on? You think about tearing it off and throwing it away. People use this bulletin board for legitimate business advertisement, but then you figure they probably have people who monitor the board and dispose of trash, and you would hate to get kicked out of the sauna before you've had sex. You are so horny right now. Excited for the prospect of getting off, you shuck your sweatpants, T-shirt, and jockstrap and stow them in a locker.

You exit the locker room into the sauna itself. The sauna is older than you remember from the last time you were here a couple of years ago. In fact, it's kind of decrepit. Some of the ancient tiling on the floor is cracked in places and totally missing in others. The wooden doors are warped, their doorknobs rusted and loose. Whatever. You're not here for the interior design. You're here to get your dick sucked.

It is still relatively early in the day, so the building is not packed. You walk past a few old men that you are not interested in and a couple who are already fucking, the bottom moaning in ecstasy as several other guys crowd around and jerk off. You go deeper into the sauna until you find an empty steam room, where you park yourself and wait for the men to come to you.

The first man who arrives cannot be a day under eighty, and his body is full of those hard brown spots that old men get for some reason. You shoo him away when he tries to kneel in front of you, and he pouts as he stands back up.

"You don't have to be so rude about it," he mumbles.

You wait a few more minutes when you hear the door open again. The second man who arrives is more your speed. He's tall and handsome, with various tattoos on his neck, pecs, and arms. He has dyed silver hair and intense eyes. He's maybe a decade older than you, but you like older men. Your husband is about the same age as he is. He could be a good candidate to help you get off, or you could wait for someone better to come along. You thought you saw a C-list musician that you know from the area out there. He could be a hot hook-up.

If you open your towel, signaling to him that you want him to fuck you, go to page 14.

If you wait for someone better to come along, go to page 11.

CHAPTER 3

YOU WANT TO WAIT FOR SOMEONE BETTER TO COME ALONG.

THE DUDE IS HOT, you'll give him that, but something about his intense demeanor is off-putting, so you decide you'll wait for someone else to come along. You've only been here for ten minutes, and there are plenty of hot guys. You shake your head at the guy, but he tries to make a move anyway.

"No, thank you," you say.

"Come on," he begs.

"I said 'no thank you'!" you reply, probably more intensely than you should have.

"Spoilsport," the man mutters, looking around to make sure no one heard you loudly reject him. He walks out of the room, slamming the wooden door behind him.

The room is awfully warm and steamy, and you were up early to help your husband pack. You're starting to get tired. You have all day to get off. Two weeks, even. You decide to take a quick nap, and you close your eyes.

You wake up some time later. You don't know how much time has passed, though if you had to guess, it probably hasn't even been an hour. You've sweated out most of the water in your body, so you decide to get up and get a drink of water. You must have stood up too fast, because suddenly you're falling. You've blacked out, but you wake up moments later on the disgusting tile floor of the sauna. Ugh, you probably have athlete's foot on your face now. You try to pull yourself up, but you can't. It's really, really warm. You call out weakly for help, and the old guy who you shooed away earlier appears at the door. You're going to have to let him suck you off, aren't you? You call for help again, and the old guy tries to open the door to save you, but he is unsuccessful. He jiggles the doorknob, but despite his best efforts, he just can't get it open. He calls for help from someone else, and a few other guys come to try to rescue you. You're going to have to suck off a lot of guys once you get your strength back, but then again, that's what you were here for.

These guys have no luck either. Eventually, the attendant from earlier comes over, and you watch as he tries in vain to open the door as well. He runs away, shouting back to you that he will call the fire department. You shouldn't have cheated on your husband. You should have stayed home, and you would have been okay. A bit horny, but okay. Your last thought as you pass out from the heat is that this is going to be so embarrassing.

The fire department gets there as quickly as it can, and they break down the door with axes. If you were alive to greet them, you'd be excited by the hunks arriving. Once the door is finally opened, the firefighters are greeted with a smell like boiled ground beef. They try in vain to revive you for about an hour.

You are dead. Go to page 31.

CHAPTER 4

YOU OPEN YOUR TOWEL, SIGNALING TO THE MAN THAT YOU'RE OPEN FOR BUSINESS.

THE MAN DROPS HIS towel, revealing his own cock, not as big as Matt's, but big enough to get you hard just looking at it. The man kneels in front of you and starts to suck you off. It feels so good. It's been too long since you got a blow job. You're about to climax, but he stops. "Keep going!" you say, admonishingly.

"Turn around," he replies. That wasn't enough foreplay, but whatever. You turn around, pressing your face against the wall. "There's lube there," you say, motioning to the small bottle you brought that has lasted you and your husband far too long. The man disregards your comment, slamming into you with more force than you were expecting. The first time it hurts, and you're worried you're bleeding. The second time hurts, but in a good way, and from there it's bliss.

A minute later, your face is pressed against the wall, and you're feeling good being slammed over and over when the man leans forward, whispering in your ear. "You wanna die?"

"What?" you ask, sure that you misheard him.

"You want to die?" He says it clearly this time.

You panic. This time, you are sure you heard it correctly. It's not a question. It's a threat. You try to pull away, but he won't let you. He reaches a hand around to the front of your neck. He's still fucking you, but it's become more forceful now. You hear a switchblade flick open, though you don't know how you recognize it as a switchblade. You're not Ponyboy. You also wonder where he was storing that knife. It's one of your last thoughts as you feel the blade cross your throat. It's like a paper cut: a quick, sharp pain, followed by nothing, and then every atom of your body hurts. You put your hand to your throat in a feeble attempt to stop the blood from pouring out, but the wound is too big. You're gasping for air that isn't coming in. You try to scream, but all you can do is gurgle. You shouldn't have cheated on your husband. You should have stayed home, and you would have been okay. A bit horny, but okay. You fall to the ground.

You are dead. Go to page 31.

CHAPTER 5

YOU DECIDE TO DOWNLOAD THE CRUISING APP THAT YOU KNOW YOU SHOULD NOT HAVE ON YOUR PHONE.

Back in the day, it was your go-to for quick, dirty sex, but you deleted it after you got married. Kind of. You deleted the app without deleting your account, and you've been back to it a few times since you got married, usually whenever your husband has refused sex, always making some lame excuse about being too tired from work or too busy with the bills or something. You're sure Matt has been on there more than a few times. Places like Denver and Chicago are sure to have lots of little torsos and asses for your husband to pick from. You go to the application store on your phone and download the app again. It takes a few minutes for it to load, and you're antsy as you wait.

A text comes in from Matt while the app is downloading. "Hey, baby, I'm boarding now, so I'm turning off my phone. I'll call you when I land. Love you!"

"Safe travels!" you type as you mutter obscenities about him leaving you horny at home and how he's forcing you to cheat on him. "Talk to you soon!"

Finally, the app downloads, and you quickly type in your username and password—the same ones that you've had since middle school—and pull up the grid. Since the last time you went on, they've changed their nudity policy, so you're immediately accosted with a variety of penises and assholes. You see long dicks and short dicks, wide dicks, and thin dicks. There are plump asses and flat asses and asses with acne and smooth asses and the scariest asses you have ever seen in your life, the holes gnarled and hairy. You could just jerk off right here to a couple of the dicks, but you're already on the app, so you might as well meet up with someone. You see a dick that you'd especially like to suck. It's about six blocks away, and it's big and uncut and perfectly veiny. You send him a "hey" and wait.

A minute goes by, then another. You are about to send him another message to see if maybe he just didn't see your first one, but you get a message from a blank profile. It says, "Hey, cutie. You want to come over? I want to suck you off."

You think for a moment. Sometimes it's easier to go with the guy who wants you over the guy who is playing hard to get. This new messenger is probably some old man, but at this point, you're desperate.

If you decide to send that second message to the guy you want to hook up with, go to page 21.

If you decide to answer the guy who messaged you first, go to page 25.

CHAPTER 6

YOU SEND THE SECOND MESSAGE TO THE GUY YOU REALLY WANTED TO HOOK UP WITH.

You wait for another moment, holding your breath, imagining that dick down your throat. Your eyes light up when you see the three dots indicating that he is responding to your message. "Hey," he responds.

"You looking?"

"Yeah, you host?"

Your husband set up cameras outside the house after a rash of break-ins in the neighborhood. He wouldn't bat an eye at you leaving and then returning after forty-five minutes, and if he asked, you would probably just say you were getting boba. If he saw that the cameras were suspiciously out for an hour, though, that would raise questions. And heaven forbid you forgot to turn it off or turned it off wrong, and he saw the owner of this wonderful penis coming up the driveway and knocking on the door. He would break up with you for sure. "No, sorry, can't host."

"Bummer, can't host either."

You think for a minute. "There's a park nearby. We could hook up in the bathroom stall." There are usually no kids at that park because there's no playground. Plus, the bathroom is kind of secluded and dingy, so you don't think there is going to be anyone there.

"Sure. See you in fifteen. Send the location."

You send him the location of the park, putting a pin where the bathroom is, and head that way, arriving in just over fifteen minutes. As you enter the park, you pass a telephone pole with a bunch of flyers pasted on it. One of them catches your eye. It is a mock-wanted poster with a picture of a zombie from an old movie. It reads, "Zombie Problems? Call Now." And then there's a number to call. At the bottom of the flyer, there is a smaller picture of a middle-aged, pasty white guy in a safari cosplay and a hideous chud fedora. Next to the photo is smaller text that reads "Rome Samuel, Zombie Hunter." What the fuck are people on?

You consider tearing it down to throw it away, but you are so horny, you do not want to delay for even a few seconds. You will get rid of it on your way out. You glance around the park, scanning for people who might ruin your fun. You don't see anyone, so you head into the bathroom.

There's already someone in the bathroom: the owner of the pretty dick you saw on your screen. He's short and muscular, with curly black hair and light brown skin. His face is cute, youthful, and mischievous, with an upturned nose and a cute grin. He is wearing a gray T-shirt and jeans that are already unbuckled. You run to him and almost slide to a kneeling position in front of his unbuckled pants, pulling on the band of his underwear to reveal your prize. It pops out of its place, already hard, and you take as much of it as you can in your mouth. It tastes clean and sweet. You are deepthroating the dick, your eyes watering and your throat gagging, when you hear a call at the door of the bathroom.

"Hey, stop! Police!" You glance over to see a police officer in the doorway. He is bulky and tall. Overweight for what you think a policeman should look like, though most police officers in this town are. He has a big bushy mustache and bad acne on his face. He is wearing a hat, but somehow you know that underneath it, he is basically bald. He runs to you and your hook-up partner, pulling his handcuffs from his belt. Fuck! If you get arrested for cruising in the bathroom while your husband is still on the plane, he's divorcing you for sure. Without a second thought, you take off running, heading out the door of the bathroom and into the larger park, ignoring the calls from the officer for you to stop. "I'm warning you! I will shoot!" That's just one of those empty threats that police officers make, right?

Then you hear a gunshot and think *Is this guy really shooting at me?* in the less-than-a-second between the shot and the impact. You feel your chest explode, and you tumble to the ground, landing face up, holding the bullet wound in your torso. You are trying to look down at your body, but you're having trouble lifting your head. You shouldn't have cheated on your husband. You should have stayed home, and you would have been okay. A bit horny, but okay. You can feel your heartbeat pumping gallons of blood out onto the park grass as you begin to fade away.

You are dead. Go to page 31.

CHAPTER 7

YOU DECIDE TO ANSWER THE GUY WHO MESSAGED YOU FIRST.

"I'D LOVE TO BE sucked off. I'll suck you off too!"

"Sounds good. Come over." He drops you a location, and you pack a few condoms and some lube and head out. You don't even ask him for a picture of himself. Sometimes the element of surprise is the hottest part.

It's about a fifteen-minute walk, and you find yourself walking from the chic gay professional neighborhood that you live in to the more upscale neighborhood where the wealthier people tend to live. You end up in front of a giant house, almost a mansion, and you knock on the front door. A man opens it. He is in his sixties and tanned within an inch of his life. He has stark white hair and whitened teeth, the same color. He is wearing a Hawaiian shirt that is open about halfway down his torso, revealing a golden chain lying in a bed of white chest hair. You swear you've seen him before.

"Welcome to my home!" he says.

"Thanks for having me," you reply. He's a bit older than you normally like, but he's hot, and you're sure you know him from somewhere. You think you may have seen him in a movie or two when you were a kid. "Were you an actor?" you ask.

"Many years ago. Now I'm more comfortable behind the camera." A rich old director! Maybe if the sex is good, he'll put you in his will. He lets you into the house, which is more beautiful on the inside than on the outside. It has mid-century modern décor with gold trim lining white walls and faux-marble tiles. It's not exactly your style, but you have to admit the old man has taste, or is at least rich enough to hire a designer. He leads you through a hallway into a large living room where a television is playing a movie. You see a glimpse of the old man on the screen, though decades younger and significantly cuter. He was a hottie in the nineties. "Let me get you a water, and then we can get started," he says.

He walks out of the room, and the movie on the TV changes to an advertisement, the weirdest one you've ever seen. It starts with flashes of scenes from different zombie movies, some new, some old, and some that you don't recognize. Then a middle-aged man appears on screen. He is dressed like he is going on safari, in tan slacks, a tan button-down shirt, and a matching fedora that sits precariously on his head. He may have been cute once, but now he's pushing fifty, pasty, and a bit pudgy. He says, "Have you been plagued by the undead? Will one of your loved ones or hated ones just not stay deceased? I'm Rome Samuel, and I'm a certified zombie hunter. I make sure the dead stay dead. If you want someone back in the grave, give me a call." A number scrolls across the bottom of the screen. *It must be some kind of advertisement for a horror movie*, you think. A bad one at that. Hopefully, it's not a movie directed by this old man.

Speaking of, the man returns, handing you a bottle of water. You open the top and take a drink. "Right this way," the old man says, leading you to a door, behind which is a staircase. You follow him down the stairs, which open into what you can only describe as a sex dungeon. The walls are covered in every sex toy imaginable, from dildos to ball gags to chastity cages to whips. In the middle of the room is a giant cross in the shape of an "X" with handcuffs and leg cuffs at each point. In front of it is a camera. It's a bit kinky for your tastes, but you're already here.

"So, what are you into?" you ask, and he answers, but for some reason, you can't process what he's saying. Nearby, you see a man kneeling on the ground, naked except for a pup mask. He is shivering, and his body is covered in welts, presumably from one of the many whips adorning the walls. You squint at him as you hear muffled noises from behind the mask. All of a sudden, you begin to feel dizzy.

"I think I should probably head out," you say, slurring your words. The man in the pup mask begins to urinate on the ground, causing an acrid smell to fill the room. Then you begin to fall. You are unconscious before you hit the ground.

When you wake up, everything is blurry for a moment, and then it comes into focus. You are cuffed to the giant cross in the middle of the room. In front of you, the old man is adjusting the camera, looking through it, and moving it a quarter of an inch at a time, presumably trying to find the perfect angle. You try to scream, but it comes out muffled, and you realize that you have the ball gag in your mouth. The pup man is in the corner still. You see a look of pity behind his mask.

"You ready to be in the movies, kid?" The old man asks, apparently having found the correct placement for the camera. "I'm thinking *Young Twunk Dismemberment Four* for a title. No wait, *Young Twunk Dismemberment Five*. I forgot about the one from last week. These go for big bucks around here, and I can never seem to keep up with the demand. So many twunks to dismember, so little time for dismembering." You try to scream out again as the old man picks up a small hand-held chainsaw and revs it up. It's the kind you have for your bushes, which freaks you out because once you put a dent in the siding of your house with it when your hand slipped the one time you tried gardening. The old man's chainsaw screeches and whirs as he brings it close to you.

You can feel tears well up in your eyes. You shouldn't have cheated on your husband. You should have stayed home, and you would have been okay. A bit horny, but okay.

"Smile for the camera. You're going to be a star." He puts the chainsaw close to your arm and drags it down. Blood splatters across your field of vision, onto the old man's face and perfectly-tailored clothes, and all over the camera. You cannot even feel the pain. You are probably in shock. "Whoops, let me clean this real quick. Don't want to miss the shot. There's only one take," he says, turning off the chainsaw and returning to the camera. You mercifully black out. You do not wake back up.

You are dead. Go to page 31.

CHAPTER 8

YOU ARE DEAD.

CORRECTION, YOU WERE DEAD. Now you're waking up, cold and naked and blind. You try to scream out, to call out your husband's name, but all that comes from your throat is a low gurgle, and your mouth is clamped shut. You sit up.

"He's alive!" you hear a voice say, but you still can't see anything. You blink and notice something behind your eyes, like contact lenses, but thicker. You reach your hand to your face, and you get a sudden scent of rotting flesh. You can think about that later; first, you need to be able to see. You fish around in your eyes for whatever is in there, and you pull them out, first the right one and then the left. It takes your eyes a minute to adjust to being able to see again, but you recognize that you're in some kind of basement that is adorned with various symbols and knick-knacks from a culture or religion you don't recognize. There are four people in the room with you, all dressed in long red robes that obscure their figures. You look down at your hands. They are green, as if you had just finished pulling up grass by hand, but they are also a deep, sickly pale. The rest of you is the same color.

You try to stand up, but your legs feel like they have been unused for weeks. You try to call out as you fall to the floor, but you remember your mouth is clamped shut. As you lie on the ground, you reach your hand into your mouth and fish around for what is keeping you from opening it. The taste of your own fingertips is horrendous, like that time you bought a chicken sandwich from the store and forgot to check the expiration date. There is a wire in your jaw on the inside of your mouth, and you can feel it under the skin. You grab hold of it and pull, and your whole body spasms with the willies as you feel the wire slip from under your skin. Once it is out, you open your mouth, though it is cramping and sore at the prospect of being opened for the first time in who-knows-how-long.

Two of the robed people run to you and help you up off the ground and back onto the concrete slab you were on when you woke up a minute ago. You remember that you are naked, but then you also remember that you have no reason to be ashamed of your body. You're a hottie. The people in the room with you drop their robes to the ground, revealing their faces and their bodies. They are naked under the robes, and, for a second, you think you are at an orgy, and you have just passed out from dehydration, and then you remember that you have not been to an orgy in years.

The first of the now-naked figures speaks. He is a white man in his fifties, a bit heavy around the waist, but overall kind of cute. He is balding and gray, and he has a small dick that sits, cold and soft, between his legs. "We are so excited to welcome you back to the land of the living. I am Brother Johnson."

"What happened?" you try to say, but again, it comes out as an unintelligible moan.

"Don't try to speak," says another naked person. This one is a Black woman, maybe thirty-five, with a bob that sits at shoulder length. She is fit and clearly works out. None of them are wearing makeup or have any tattoos. "Sister David, please get our friend some water," she says to the other woman, an old granny type with long gray hair and a saggy pale body.

"Yes, Sister Williams." The old lady runs off, bouncing back and forth on her legs like old people do when they try to run.

"Are we sure they can drink water?" says the other man, a hunky guy in his early twenties who you are pretty sure is South Indian. He has abs for days and a nice uncut dick.

"I am not sure, Brother Thevar. It can't hurt to try," says Brother Johnson. Sister David returns with a glass of water and hands it to you. You take a drink but immediately spit it out. Something about the taste is repulsive to you. "I guess they can't."

"Who are you?" you try to say, but still can't form the words. The sound and cadence are enough for the others to figure out what you are saying.

Sister Williams speaks. "We are The Church of Life Again [a cult, surely], and we have been trying for months to find a suitable candidate for resurrection. We have been trying and trying, and some of our number had begun to lose faith."

"We used to have a dozen churchgoers," interjects Brother Thevar.

Sister Williams continues. "But tonight, we finally succeeded. So, bad news, you died. It was a few weeks ago, judging by the smell. Good news, you are alive again, thanks to us."

"Now that we have been successful, we can try this again!" exclaims Brother Johnson. "We have cured death."

"Oh death, where is thy sting?" asks Sister David rhetorically. "Oh grave, where is thy victory?"

Brother Thevar speaks next. "We're certain that your bodily functions will be restored soon enough. Well, at least your speech and your muscle memory. Unfortunately, all of your blood has been replaced by embalming fluid. We don't think it will be a problem for everyday life, but like, your heart is not beating." It's true. Normally, as you go about your day, you don't think about your heart beating, but now that it's not there, you can feel its absence. You have no blood in your body, but whatever fluid is in your veins and arteries is not pumping.

All of this death stuff is really hard to process, and you sit back on the table. You put your hand up to your head, but once again, you smell an overwhelming rot and move your hands back away from your head. Suddenly, you are hungry. Hungrier than you have ever been in your life. “Hungry,” you try to say, but it just comes out as a grunt.

Sister Williams knows what you meant, and she runs over to the corner where a purse sits among a pile of clothes that the cultists had clearly discarded in favor of the robes they were wearing. She rifles through her bag, pulling out a bag of nacho cheese tortilla chips. She runs back and hands them to you. You try to open them, but your dexterity has not quite returned yet. Brother Thevar helps you open the bag, and you grab a handful of the chips, shoving them in your face. You cough as the taste, or lack thereof, hits you, and you spit them back out. It’s like eating cardboard: fully flavorless and difficult for you to even keep in your mouth, much less swallow. You are so hungry. You stumble to your feet and look at the cultists in front of you. Suddenly, Brother Thevar is looking tasty, and not in a sexual way. You’d even take a bite out of Sister David, even though she has to be at least seventy-five and you’ve never much gone for women your own age, much less old ladies. These cultists have already given you the gift of life. Would you also want to take the gift of sustenance from them, too?

If you decide that you are so hungry you could eat a whole cult, go to page 37.

If you decide that cultists are not on the menu, go to page 41.

CHAPTER 9

YOU ARE SO HUNGRY, YOU COULD EAT A WHOLE CULT.

You laugh to yourself, wishing you could tell the cult the funny joke, but it's not like they'd understand or find it as hilarious as you do. You take a deep breath (shocked that you can breathe at all), and you let the hunger take over. It drives your body like you aren't even there. Brother Johnson is first. You dive at him, still a little unsteady, and sink your teeth into his neck. The man screams as you bite down, feeling his blood begin to run into your mouth. It's the best thing you've ever tasted: better than honey or strawberry milkshakes or that spicy ranch dressing you like. The warm liquid fills your mouth, and you swallow it; then you use your teeth to tear a large chunk out of the man's flesh to get more. The other cultists run to you to try to get you to stop, but you throw them off with ease. You were somewhat strong in life, but now, in death, you're basically a superhero. Or a supervillain. Sister David is out of commission immediately. When you throw her off of you, she slams her head into the wall and then crumples to the ground. She may be dead. If not, she will be soon.

The other two are a different story. Sister Williams is strong, despite being short, and Brother Thevar is bigger than you. They try to hold you down, but you're stronger than them both combined. You grab Brother Thevar's arm and twist it behind his head. You keep twisting and twisting, ignoring the pops and the screams, and then the arm tears off, like a drumstick being pulled from a rotisserie chicken. Blood sprays everywhere. You try to remember if your death involved blood like this, but you can't think about anything right now. You slam the arm into Sister Williams. It throws her to the floor. You grab the broken humerus, sharp and jagged, and slam it into Sister Williams' chest.

When you straighten up, you notice that Sister David is conscious again, dragging her feeble body away from you. "Please!" she says. "We saved you."

Her pleas fall on deaf ears. You lift her off the ground, holding her head in one hand and her shoulder in the other. You get a grip on the top of her head, and you twist. Sister David's eyes bulge, then fill with blood. You hear snapping, indicating she is dead, but you don't stop your twisting. You twist until you feel the head pop off the body. Then you step back and survey your handiwork. The cultists all lay dead. Now it's time to eat.

You finish off Brother Johnson first, consuming flesh and skin and blood and even hair, until all that is left is blood-covered bones.

You'll lick the rest of that off later. You eat Brother Thevar's arm next as an appetizer to Sister Williams. You had to pull it out of her chest anyway. You gobble down his massive bicep and triceps, which are a bit chewy and tough, and then you turn to Sister Williams, eating every bit of her too, until the only distinguishing feature between her and Brother Johnson is that he was a few inches taller. You wonder what brains taste like, so you crack Sister David's skull open against the wall, the same way you did to a coconut when you and Matt went on vacation to Hawaii. The brains spill on the floor, and you eat them by the mouthful. They are amazing as well, better than blood even. You go back to Brother Johnson and Sister Williams, eating their brains too, and then you finish off the rest of Sister David.

You saved the best for last. Poor, hot, armless Brother Thevar. You start with his face, eating his lips, then his nose, then his eyes, then his ears, then you work your way down his body, eating enormous muscle after enormous muscle. You tear off pieces of his dick as if you were eating a licorice rope and feel his balls pop in your mouth as you bite down. Once you are done, and the cultists are only identifiable by their dental records, you stand up.

You are still hungry. Go to page 41.

CHAPTER 10

YOU ARE SO HUNGRY, YOU COULD EAT ANYTHING.

YOU LEAVE THE BASEMENT, emerging onto the street. It's dark outside, which is good, because you are still naked, but also not good, because you are starving, and no one is around for you to eat. You glance at the street around you. You know where you are. You're only a few miles away from home. You want to go home, but you are so hungry. You start to run, naked, through the streets of your city. You realize you are faster than you were in life, not quite as fast as a superhero with super speed, but faster than any human. Once you satisfy this hunger, you may be able to make a career for yourself in the Olympics. You're making good progress when you trip on something you didn't see and go flying across the sidewalk, scraping parts of your body you never thought you would scrape against concrete.

"Fuck you!" you hear. You turn back to see what you tripped over. A homeless man is lying in the street, covered in blankets. "I'm sleeping here!"

You pick yourself up, and the homeless man is getting up. For the first time, your own stench of rotting flesh is overpowered by the smell of urine. “Naked faggot,” the old man mutters. He has four brown teeth spaced out throughout his mouth and a yellowed beard and mustache. Everything else is covered by layers of clothes with holes in them. “You faggots just think you own the whole sidewalk.”

You are so hungry. You could easily just eat this hate-crime-ing hobo right here and now, but he smells bad, and you want to be home.

If you decide to eat this hobo, go to page 43.

If you decide to go home, go to page 45.

CHAPTER 11

YOU DECIDE TO EAT THE HOMELESS MAN.

He smells awful, but you are so hungry. You lunge at him, tearing off his clothes like they're a candy wrapper. Finally, you encounter flesh. Suddenly, you're met with a wave of the rancid smell of shit and piss. You don't care. You're just so hungry. You dig into his stomach, tasting the sweet blood as it fills your mouth. You reach through the wound in his belly and grab his intestines, slurping them into your mouth like spaghetti. The man has soiled himself, but you keep eating. You've consumed all of his organs in his torso, and you keep eating. You smash his skull against the pavement again and again until his brains are pouring out on the sidewalk. You're so hungry that you don't even use your hands to eat them, kneeling like a dog and licking them off the ground, feeling the cool night air against your exposed asshole. Hearing the sound of a police siren, you take a final bite of the brains and then look up.

"What's going on here?" you hear, and in the dark, you can't make out the policeman's face. His silhouette is tall and bulky, and you think that he is probably meatier and cleaner than the hobo you're eating, so, running on all fours, you bound towards him and leap at him like a frog jumping to eat a fly or a lion pouncing on its prey. You tackle the officer to the ground, and hear his head crack against the sidewalk. Before, this might have sickened you, but now it only makes your stomach rumble in hunger and anticipation.

Up close, you can make out the cop's features. He is overweight and has a big bushy mustache and bad acne on his face. You may have seen him before, but then again, all police officers in your town look like this. You blame Tom Selleck.

You tear the man's shirt open, exposing a weirdly hairless chest, like he waxes. You pull your arm back for a head start and slam your fingers into his chest, breaking through with ease. It's as easy as a child reaching into their birthday cake for a handful of frosting. You grab a chunk of the man's flesh and bring it to your mouth. In the blue and red light, you consume the policeman whole. When you've finished him off, his skeleton is stripped, but you are still hungry. You go back to the hobo and finish eating, leaving some of the nastier parts.

You are still hungry. Go to page 45.

CHAPTER 12

YOU DECIDE TO GO HOME.

YOU WERE ABOUT HALFWAY home when you encountered the homeless man, so it does not take you long at all to get to your house after that. You stand outside the beautiful home you once shared with Matt. He's probably so sad about your death. You just imagine him lying in bed, crying over losing you, vowing to never marry again, never have sex again (it's not as if he wanted to have it much when you were alive). He will just spend the rest of his days in mourning. If he were more flamboyant, he might even wear a veil, but flamboyance has never been his thing.

From the outside sidewalk, you notice that the light is on upstairs, but the rest of the house is dark. This means he's home. Good, he shouldn't be going out with you so recently dead anyway. You stop at the door, trying to remember the passkey to unlock it. You certainly don't have your keys on you. What was it? Then you remember. 1218. Your birthday. Your husband always insisted on making the code your birthdate. You enter it in, praying that your husband hasn't changed it since your untimely death. To your relief, the door opens, and you head immediately to the stairs. You take the steps two at a time and stop outside the door, excited to surprise Matt. You open the door quietly, but as it opens, you hear a commotion in the room.

Your jaw drops as you see what is going on. On your bed, your husband is lying naked, a tablet in one hand and his massive cock in the other. "Yeah, baby," he says, alternating between looking at the device in his hand and letting his eyes roll back into his head. He's not seen you yet.

"Let me see it," you hear from the tablet, and he turns it around (your husband was never very good at technology. He probably does not even know how to switch to the back camera). Your husband still hasn't noticed you, but the guy on the tablet does, making eye contact with you once he is facing you. He screams. "Monster!"

"Yeah, it is!" Matt says in a sexy voice. His eyes are closed, and you know he's close to climax because his leg is twitching like it does every time he comes.

"No! There's someone in your room!" the man shrieks. Your husband opens his eyes and sees you.

"Baby?" he says. It's the second person he's called that in so many seconds. He fumbles with the tablet, managing to hang up with the person he was masturbating with.

You stare at him, looking dead into his eyes, your excitement to see him immediately replaced by fury.

"I was just—"

"Doing mutual masturbation on a tablet, something you never did with me in our five years of marriage because you were afraid someone was going to take screenshots and send them to your boss!" is what you would have said if you were able to talk in more than grunts and groans, and moans. Instead, you just glare at him with a knowing look that tells him he's royally fucked up.

"It's not what it seems like."

You make a face that you hope communicates, "Well then, what is it? Because it seems like you immediately moved on from me and started to spice up your relationship with your new man in ways that you never did with me."

His face falls, and you know that you were successful in getting your point across. "Fine, that is what it is. You'd been dead for two weeks, and I was in mourning. I just wanted to get off, and you weren't around to get me off. I don't even know how you're standing here now. They called me when I got to Dallas and told me you had died. I identified your body. I planned your funeral. You are dead."

Two weeks? You are pissed. You thought for sure you had been dead longer than that. It would have been unforgivable if he had moved on in the six months you thought you were gone, but your body was still warm, and he was having a jerk sesh with some rando on video call.

You move across the room, and he tries to stand up, but you are faster than him now. Stronger than him. You grab him, gripping his naked shoulder and slamming him against the wall. He lets out a pained moan, but you feel something touching your chest. You look down. It's his dick, almost eleven inches hard, poking you. Something about the roughness of being slammed into a wall has aroused him. Damn, you should have done some more impact play when you were alive. You grab the penis with your free hand, and he sucks in air through his teeth.

"Yes!" he moans, and you set him down gently. This is long overdue. Maybe if this had happened two weeks ago, you would still be alive. You kneel in front of your husband and take his dick in your mouth. Normally, you can only get a few inches in your mouth, but being dead has completely destroyed your gag reflex. You push your mouth up to the base of the cock and hold it there. "Oh, baby, I missed you so much, baby," he groans out.

You use your tongue to wrap around the penis, and you can feel him spurting down your throat. Bullshit. He didn't miss you. He immediately moved on to some twink whore that he didn't even have the decency to sleep with in a different bed than the one you shared. You are still hungry.

You bite down on the penis and hear a *squick* as it detaches from Matt's body. It seems to take him a few seconds to figure out what just happened. Then he lets out a howl. You try to swallow the penis whole, but it's difficult. It takes three or four tries to get it down, but you send the monstrous thing down to your stomach. All the while, Matt is screaming in front of you, the stump where his member used to be spraying blood mixed with the semen he had been coming moments ago.

He screams and screams, and you use the shock of the moment to turn him around. Your face is now directly in front of his hairy, plump ass. You so loved eating it while you were alive, and it is going to be even tastier now. You chomp down on the left buttock, taking a big chunk of it off. Your husband just screams louder. He's still alive as you make your way up his back, but by the time you turn him back around to eat the front side of him, he's dead from the loss of blood. You consume the love of your life, piece by piece, until the only thing that is left is his bones. It's only about fifteen minutes from first bite to completely stripped bones, and when you are done, for a moment, you are satiated.

You stand up and look at yourself in the floor-length mirror you used to masturbate onto when you were alive. It is the first time you've seen yourself since you woke up, and you despair at the decay. You used to be hot. So hot, in fact, that your husband kind of ignored the fact that you were admittedly a deadbeat loser. You never held a job for more than a few months, and when you died, it had been years since you had worked at all. You didn't cook, you didn't clean, and you certainly didn't give particularly amazing head. But you did have your body: tight abs and pecs flush against a tall, slim frame; a pretty penis that was just enough above average to be desirable without being unwieldy; a face like chiseled marble, reminiscent of the statue of David and eternally youthful, despite your careening towards middle age (you wonder if you will continue to age as a member of the undead, or if you're stuck at thirty-two); and a mop of curly dark hair that has never once shown any signs of receding.

Now, you're nothing short of disgusting. The first thing you notice is your penis, shriveled and pruny, like your fingers after a long bath. There is no blood flow to it, and even with your late husband's enormous member halfway down your esophagus, you never felt the telltale tingle of the beginning of an erection. You were always more of a bottom anyway, but you are going to miss jerking off. You were good at it.

Every inch of skin on your body is sickly pale, and the places that were normally red or blue with veins and arteries are now green and yellow. You press your finger on your pec for a few seconds and then move it away, remembering a trick a nurse friend taught you about checking for blood flow. Instead of the blood rushing to that spot as it should, your fingerprint stays indented in your chest. You watch it for a moment, wondering when the mark will go away. It does not, so you turn around to look at your backside. It is worse than the front. Your back is mottled, and on your once-perky left buttock is a wound about the size of a baseball. You grab it, trying to get a better look when you see something that makes you begin to feel sick to your stomach. There are white, juicy maggots crawling in your flesh. They writhe and wiggle in your left butt cheek. The worst part is, you can't even feel them moving around. There could be a hundred more anywhere in your body. Suddenly, you are hungry again at the sight of moving flesh, and you reach down and pluck one of the little worms from its home in your backside. You hold it up to the light; its body is almost transparent. You never would have done this before, but now you don't even think twice as you put it in your mouth and bite down, feeling it explode between your teeth like a grape. Then you spit it out. Just like the chips, it is basically inedible. You look at the crushed worm on the floor of the house you once called home and suddenly feel a bit sad. You apologize to it and promise its siblings that are still in your asscheek that they will have a home with you.

Suddenly, your stomach lurches. You ate so much flesh, and you never stopped to wonder where it was going. Of course, there's no stomach acid left in there, so your body can't break your enormous meals down. You start to heave, and then you vomit, spraying chunks of flesh and gallons of blood all over the bed. It's okay. You aren't tired, and you don't think you ever will be again, so the bed may as well be your vomit bin. You puke again, this time spewing gray matter against your wall. Your husband was so smart; now look at those brains. You retch a final time and dump gallons more viscera onto the carpet. You feel a hitch in your throat and cough a few times, finally spitting up your husband's penis, fully intact since you had swallowed it whole.

You are finally done losing your guts when you hear sirens outside. You glance down at your husband's tablet that is face up on the floor. You had not heard it dinging earlier, but now you check, and there are a dozen or more texts from someone named Robbie.

"Babe, is everything alright?"

"Baby? Who was that?"

"Matt, I'm scared. Call me, please."

"Just a text. Let me know you're alive."

"Matt, I'm gonna call the police in five minutes if I don't hear back from you."

"Matt, please respond."

"Matt, the police are on their way."

It's time for you to go, but you can't keep running around the city with your dick out, so you root through your closet quickly for your favorite gray hoodie and a pair of sweatpants. Then you find an old pair of tennis shoes (having been wearing your nice pair when you died) and slip them on. You say one final goodbye to your husband's guts and viscera, grab his wallet off the dresser and remove a stack of bills, open the side window of the house, and jump out of it, landing on your feet. You hide in the bushes, watching a handful of police officers swarm your house.

You hear one of them scream out. "What the fuck!" He comes back down the stairs and runs to his car. His hands are shaking, and you can tell by the darkness on the front of his uniform that he's pissed himself. He grabs his radio from the car. "Send backup to our location. It's a slaughterhouse in here." You could kill him, but you wouldn't have time to eat him, considering his friends are still up there. You are hungry again. You have a few options to satisfy your hunger. You could eat random people or just go a few blocks and break into another house. That's a bit risky, but probably the easiest. The next option is to be more targeted about it. There are people in your life who definitely deserve to be eaten, and you're feeling a bit petty. Your last option is that you could be a hero. There are a lot of bad people out on the streets, and you could eat them. You could be the killer that only kills people who deserve it, like that one premium cable show you never watched because there weren't enough naked men. You should probably leave your house soon, so it's time to decide.

If you want to break into random houses and eat people, go to page 97.

If you want to be a hero and only eat bad people, like Dexter, but for zombies, go to page 123.

If you want to be petty and try to eat people who have wronged you in your life, go to page 63.

CHAPTER 13

YOU CHEATED.

YOU ARE NOT SUPPOSED to be here. You cheated at this adventure, just like you cheated on your husband. You're a dirty cheater. Or maybe you're just dumb. You were never very good at this kind of game. Following instructions can be hard for you sometimes. I guess it's possible that you've expended all of your other options, and, desperately searching for a happy ending, you went through and read every single page of this book, which brought you here. I hate to break it to you, but happy endings aren't real life. In real life, people die. They get shot, they get disemboweled, they get their throats slit, or they die of carbon monoxide poisoning, and sure, sometimes they die in freak sauna accidents. And even if they come back to life, they always die again eventually. Every time.

But you got this far, so here's your goddamn happy ending.

You wake up, feeling more refreshed than you have in a long time. Your sense of smell is no longer covered in the stench of rotting human flesh, and you can smell beautiful, sweet flowers. You look around. You're in a bed of roses, but there are no thorns.

Just petals, soft and pleasant against your naked body, which is whole again. You can see the veins running through your hands, and your heart is beating. You are outside, but you are not cold, despite being naked. The temperature is seventy degrees, exactly the temperature you set your home thermostat to, and there is not a cloud in the sky.

"Babe," you hear the voice of your husband, alive again (or still. I don't know how far you got in the rest of the book).

"What happened?" you ask.

Matt reaches over, placing his hand pleasantly on your chest, playing with your chest hair. "A rainbow unicorn came down from the sky and said that every good person in human history was now alive and immortal, and every bad person in human history never existed. Since we're both alive, we must have been good people."

"Must have," you say, lying back, feeling a sense of happiness and contentment that you have not felt in a long time. Maybe ever.

"Wanna have sex?" Matt asks. You nod and roll over on him. Because this is a perfect world, you don't even need any lube. Your asshole is self-lubricating, and you slide onto his enormous dick in pleasure without a bit of pain.

There you go, motherfucker: a happy ending, full of beds of roses, rainbow unicorns, and self-lubricating buttholes. Happy now?

Now go back and do it the right way. Go to page 1.

CHAPTER 14

YOU WAKE UP IN THE BASEMENT AGAIN.

"WELCOME BACK," SAYS SISTER David. You sit up. It's easier this time.

"What? Where?" you try to say, but you still can't talk. Damn cultists can't figure out how to resurrect someone with their Broca's area intact.

Sister Williams understands what you're saying again. She'd make a good zombie interpreter. "When we heard on the news that there was a rash of violent crimes and then a weeks-old body discovered, we figured it was you. Brother Thevar and I snuck into the morgue and retrieved your body. We've been trying since we resurrected you to replicate the process with other corpses, but so far we've had no luck at all."

"No luck at all," echoes Sister David.

Sister Williams continues. "We figured we would try again with you, since it worked the first time, and, sure enough, it did. You're alive again. The first un-un-undead in recorded history."

"We took the liberty of putting you back together," says Brother Johnson.

"Ahem," says Brother Thevar.

"Brother Thevar took the liberty of putting you back together," Brother Johnson corrects himself. You stumble to your feet, looking at your body; new stitches and sutures are covering the places where you were killed last time. You glance around the room. The cultists are naked again. You wonder if they ever get cold or weirded out by each other's bodies. The hunger hits you again, this time more powerful than it was last time. You can't control yourself, despite what the cultists have done for you. Your "get out of hell free card" is about to expire.

Brother Johnson is first. You dive at him, still a little unsteady, and sink your teeth into his neck. The man screams as you bite down, feeling his blood begin to run into your mouth, and you swallow it; then you use your teeth to tear a large chunk out of the man's flesh to get more. The other cultists run to you to try to get you to stop, but you throw them off with ease. Sister David is out of commission immediately. When you throw her off of you, she slams her head into the wall. She falls to the ground. She may be dead. If not, she will be soon.

The other two are a different story. Sister Williams is strong, despite being short, and Brother Thevar is bigger than you. They try to hold you down, but you're stronger than them both combined. You grab Brother Thevar's arm and twist it behind his head. You keep twisting and twisting, and ignoring the pops and the screams, and then the arm pops off, like a drumstick being pulled from a rotisserie chicken. Blood sprays everywhere. You try to remember if your last death involved blood like this, but you can't think about anything right now. You slam the arm into Sister Williams. It throws her to the floor. You grab the broken humerus, sharp and jagged, and you slam it into Sister Williams' chest.

When you straighten up, you notice that Sister David is conscious again, dragging her feeble body away from you. "Please!" she says. "We saved you twice!" Her pleas fall on deaf ears. You lift her off the ground, holding her head in one hand and her shoulder in the other. You get a grip on the top of her head and twist. Sister David's eyes bulge, then fill with blood. You hear snapping, indicating she is dead, but you don't stop your twisting. You twist until you feel the head pop off the body. You survey your handiwork. The cultists all lay dead. Now it's time to eat.

You finish off Brother Johnson first, consuming flesh and skin and blood and even hair, until all that is left is blood-covered bones. You'll lick the rest of that off later. You eat Brother Thevar's arm next as an appetizer to Sister Williams. You had to pull it out of her chest anyway. You gobble down his massive bicep and triceps, which are a bit chewy and tough, and then you turn to Sister Williams, eating every bit of her too, until the only distinguishing feature between her and Brother Johnson is that he is a few inches taller. You crack open Sister David's skull against the wall, the same way you did with a coconut when you and Matt went on vacation to Hawaii. The brains spill on the floor, and you eat them by the mouthful, then you go back to Brother Johnson and Sister Williams, eating their brains too. You finish off the rest of Sister David next.

You saved the best for last—poor, hot, armless Brother Thevar. You start with his face, eating his lips, then his nose, then his eyes, and his ears, then you work your way down his body, eating enormous muscle after enormous muscle. Once you are done, and the cultists are only identifiable by their dental records, you stand up. You see a pile of the cultist's clothes in the corner and root through them for Brother Thevar's clothes. He is about the same size as you, though slightly more muscular. You slip a pair of dirty boxers over your legs, then pull on his T-shirt and finally a pair of jeans that he was wearing. They're a bit loose on you, so you pull the belt tighter. You grab a jacket that probably belonged to Sister Williams, but you don't particularly care. You wish there were a mirror to see what you look like, but for all the cultish décor, there is not a single reflective surface.

You go up the stairs and back onto the streets of the city. You don't know where to go, but you are still hungry. Your body takes you back to your house. You run across the city, panting. You do not encounter anyone on the way. You would eat any homeless person you came across now, but it's late at night, and with the number of deaths in the city the last few weeks, everyone is probably hiding. You arrive at your house, but the police tape is still covering it. You just want to be safe at home, but you can't, because you ate your husband and then vomited his guts (and yours) across the entire bedroom. You need to eat something, and you have some options. You already did one of the following, but the other two should be fine, right?

If you want to break into random houses and eat people, go to page 97.

If you want to be a hero and only eat bad people, like Dexter, but for zombies, go to page 123.

If you want to be petty and try to eat people who have wronged you in your life, go to page 63.

CHAPTER 15

YOU DECIDE TO BE PETTY AND TRY TO EAT PEOPLE WHO HAVE WRONGED YOU IN YOUR LIFE.

YOUR LIFE SUCKED. WELL, it didn't. In fact, it was kind of cushy as far as gay dudes' lives go, but that doesn't mean you didn't have your fair share of enemies. You're already dead, so you don't have much to live for, and you're going to have to eat something (someone), so you might as well eat the people who made your life a living hell. You make a list for yourself of who you are going to eat. Your dad is obviously at the top of your list, for all the times he called you a faggot, all the times he slapped you around a bit when you didn't perform masculinity for him, and for that time he broke your first boyfriend's arm when he found the two of you together in bed after your first sexual encounter. He's for sure getting eaten.

Number two is your high school bully, who you know lives nearby. You once saw him grilling outside on his lawn a few blocks away. He tried to cheerily greet you, seemingly having forgotten that he gave you a literal swirly sophomore year and senior year, told the teacher that you had tried to plagiarize a paper, almost keeping you from graduating. You're going to tear his smug little face off and swallow it down like a pancake.

You rack your brains for another victim, and then, looking at your boring backyard, it comes to you: City Councilman Dan Danielson. That smug bastard ruined your chances of having an in-ground pool. You begged and begged Matt for a pool. You could afford it. Well, *he* could afford it. But there was a problem at City Hall with the permits. They were taking forever to be approved. Something about ground stability and flooding. You didn't even really know what the hold up was, but you were committed to getting your pool, so you decided to use your sexuality and charm as a tool to get what you wanted. You had read on the city hall website that Councilman Dan Danielson was an out and proud gay man, and you'd even seen him on the app once, though you would never have told that to anyone. You marched into his office one day in the outfit you had used to seduce your husband, looking to trade a favor for a favor. He was an older man with gray hair, veneers, and wrinkles around his eyes. He was cute enough, but at this point, you would suck off Abraham Lincoln to get that pool.

You sat down on the chair in front of his desk, and he asked what he could do for you. You put your feet up on the desk, knowing that he could see down the shorts you were wearing to catch a glimpse of your dick (you, of course, weren't wearing any underwear), and explained what it was that you wanted. You offered an exchange. If he got those papers pushed through, you would help him out, too. You bit your lip, and his face flushed. He ran to the door and closed it, pulling down the curtain. Within moments, you were sucking his dick. It was small and sad, and he didn't even get hard as you pulled your lips around it. You even tried fingering his asshole, which made him gasp, but didn't get him erect. Eventually, he came soft, and you wiped your mouth and left, reminding him about that paperwork. A few days later, a note arrived at your house that you picked up before your husband could see. It was from the councilman, and he said that he looked you up and found out that you were married and that he does not have sex with married men. He was denying your paperwork, and if he ever saw you on that app again, he would tell your husband that you sucked his dick. You've held a grudge ever since, and so he is going on the list of people you are eating.

You'll have to add more people to your list later. Right now, you're hungry.

If your daddy issues win out and you go after your father first, go to page 66.

If you want to return that swirly, but instead of a toilet, his head is going in your gut, go to page 75.

If you decide that the councilman is going to go swimming in your gut, go to page 71.

CHAPTER 16

YOUR DADDY ISSUES WIN OUT.

SORRY, DAD, YOU DESERVE it. He's in a retirement home nearby, his alcohol-induced dementia having made it impossible for him to live alone despite being barely sixty-five. Your mom took care of him until a couple of years ago, when she passed away due to a heart attack, at which point you signed him over to the state and had him dumped in a nursing home. You haven't visited that entire time, but you know where it is. It's a few miles from you. You set off on foot towards the nursing home. It only takes you about thirty minutes to get there, and at this point, the sun is rising. It's the first morning of the rest of your afterlife. The building is on the new side, all one floor, but rather large. Your mom must have put away a decent amount of money for the state to send your dad here to live out his days.

You go through the building's front entrance and up to the front desk. A heavyset woman with too-long nails greets you. "You here to see someone?" You nod. "You can't go in there if you're sick. Are you sick?" You shake your head. "You look it," she says. You don't care. You ignore her and head down the hallway, watching various nurses working with old people, each one looking tastier than the next. You remember your dad is somewhere in the 100s hallway. You got an email once with his room number. You start peeking in each room, looking for the bastard who spawned you. Finally, you find him in room 117.

Your old man has gone downhill since the last time you saw him. He sits in a wheelchair, dressed in pajama pants and a T-shirt covered in drool. He's barely 100 pounds, and you can smell that he's shat his pants. His mouth hangs open, and spit runs into his recently shaved face, even though you had never seen him without a beard in your whole life before this moment.

"Kiddo?" he asks, his eyes lighting up. "That you?" You nod. "Oh, good, some crazy lady dressed like a nurse told me you were dead. I didn't believe her. I have been trying to get them to let me call you. Have you seen your mom?" You shake your head. "I thought she was around here somewhere, but I haven't seen her in a few days." It has been over two years since your mom's death, and longer since he's seen her, but apparently, the alcohol that fucked up his brain makes it hard for him to be able to tell time. You stare at the old man. He's evil, but it would just be sad to eat him now. Plus, there's not a lot of meat on his bones anyway. You turn around to leave, but the old man says, "You leaving, kid?" You turn back around and nod. "Come visit your old man more often."

You nod again, and then you leave. You haven't forgiven him, but also, he spends his whole life not remembering where he is, shitting his pants day in and day out. This is punishment enough.

On the way out, you hear a woman's voice in a room nearby. "Fuck you, old man!"

"Help!" you hear an old man's voice say. You decide to check and see what is going on, knowing it's probably some confused patient unhappy with getting washed up or something. You could not have been more wrong. An old man is sprawled on the ground, naked, and a nurse's assistant is standing over him. She has one of those tan belts they use to help transfer the patients, and she is whipping the old man over and over again with it. You run over to her, stopping her before she can hit him again. You pick her up by the back of the neck and slam her into the wall. She's unconscious before she can scream. You apply pressure to the back of her neck until you feel her skull begin to crumble under the weight of your hand. Her head pops like a balloon, splattering brains and skull fragments all over the wall and floor.

You walk over to the old man whose expression shows that he probably does not know what is going on. You help him gently to the bed. "Thank you, sonny," he says. There is a large dresser next to his bed, and you dig in it for some clothes and help the man get dressed, then you lift him into his wheelchair and wheel it out to the hallway so you can feast.

"See ya later," he says as you return to the room. You pick up a piece of brain from the ground and eat it. It tastes so good. You strip naked so as not to mess up your clothes any more than they already are and get started on consuming the nurse from head to toe. Then you dress again and leave the room, waving to the old man as you pass.

At the front desk, the receptionist says, "Did you have a nice visit?" You keep your body angled away from her and grunt out an affirmative. Then you disappear into the night. You are still hungry, so you decide to eat another one of your enemies.

If you decide to eat your high school bully, go to page 75.

If you decide to eat the councilman next, go to page 71.

CHAPTER 17

THAT COUNCILMAN IS GOING SWIMMING.

In your gut. You wouldn't want to deprive the man of a nice swim, even though he deprived you of your own pool a few years ago. You walk through the morning streets and head toward his office. City hall is not busy; it's too early in the morning for that. You walk right through the metal detectors. There's no weapon on you except for your teeth. City hall is not particularly big—you don't live in New York. It's a couple of floors, and it also houses the city library. You know where the councilman's office is, since you've sucked his dick before. You head straight to his office and burst through the door. The councilman is at his desk. His face is red, and his eyes are rolled back in his head. *Is he masturbating?* you think to yourself.

"What the fuck?" he asks as he sees you.

From below his desk, a young man's face pops up. He looks younger than twenty-five, maybe younger than twenty. He has rosy cheeks and that awful perm that everyone his age has. "Who is that, daddy?"

"Shh, some loser who sucked me off in here once. I rejected him because he was married. Go back to blowing me; I'll take care of this." The councilman doesn't seem to recognize that he is about to be eaten alive.

"You've had other guys in here?" the young man pouts.

"Way before I met you, baby. And you give better head." He looks at you. "What do you want? You still aren't getting your pool." You just stare at him, disgusted. "I'm going to tell your husband that you cheated on him." You want to say a dozen things to him, none of them pleasant, but you obviously can't, so you just lunge at him. You pick him up out of his chair before he can move. He is pantsless and his flaccid dick swings towards you. He climaxes, and, for the second time in this office in as many years, you are covered in his jizz. You are about to kill him when you feel something on your back. The demon twink from under the desk is on top of you, and he has one arm wrapped around your throat and is hitting you with his other fist. You drop the councilman and thrash around the room, trying to throw the little asshole from your shoulders. You succeed, and he crashes to the ground unconscious. You'll eat him next. For now, you return your attention to the councilman. He has crawled under his desk, and you lumber over to it and crouch down, making eye contact with him.

You are about to drag him from under the desk when the door swings open again. A bunch of security guards, at least four that you can see, burst in, and you stand up, distracted from the councilman. The security guards all have their guns trained on you, and one of them yells, "Fire!" A barrage of gunfire comes your way, and your body dances as you are peppered with bullets. When the gunfire stops, you are still standing. The bullet holes riddling your body hurt, but they haven't put you out of commission. You are not sure if you can survive another round of gunfire, though, so you leap over the desk and push through the guards, sending them flying. Then you race out of the building before the guards can follow you.

You need to hide. Go to page 89.

CHAPTER 18

YOU'RE GOING TO RETURN THAT SWIRLY, BUT INSTEAD OF A TOILET, HIS HEAD IS GOING IN YOUR GUT.

As you make your way to where the bully lives, you try to remember his name. Gary? Gavin? Sadly, you can't even remember the name of the person who caused you so much misery in your lifetime. That's okay, you'll remember how he tastes. You make your way to his house, which is not far from where you lived with your husband. As you go, you remember back to high school and your many bad interactions with him that helped him find his place at the top of your shitlist.

The first negative interaction was during freshman year. You had just come out as gay and had thankfully been accepted into the cool gay clique (probably because you lied and said you had sucked a dick in middle school). At your school, there were cool gays, and there were lame gays. The lame gays went to GSA and organized protests and made posters with drawings of anime characters explaining pronouns. The cool gays fucked older men on cruising apps and went into sex shops with their fake IDs and had several simultaneous substance addictions at any given time (you drank vodka heavily and smoked like a chimney). The lame gays were totally available for bullying, and the cool gays were off-limits. Anyways, freshman year, you saw one of the lame gays, a chubby little twerp named Anton (whose name was far cooler than he was), walking down the hallways, holding one of the posters he had made in GSA. You didn't like how the posters they made in GSA always highlighted how lame some gay people could be, so you called him a faggot under your breath. The kid gave you a dirty look, but Greg, who at that point was on the junior football team, overheard it. He stormed up to you, attempting to be intimidating. "Hey, quit saying that," he said, as if he had any say in what language you used.

"Say what?" you replied.

"Faggot," he whispered.

You gasped. "How dare you?" You ran to the nearest teacher to tell him that this straight asshole had said a slur. Of course, your school was homophobic, so they wouldn't punish him.

The next time you had a bad encounter with Gabe was during sophomore year. You were smoking in the bathroom when the bell rang, and a few kids entered. George and his buddies were there, as was some little freshman whose name you didn't know. The kid looked at you smoking and said, "Can you put that out? I have asthma." You scoffed. How dare he? You took a drag of the cigarette and blew it in the kid's face, causing him to start coughing. Then you laughed because it was funny.

"Not cool, dude," said one of your bully's friends, taking the kid out of the bathroom, leaving you with Grant, who did not look happy.

"What the fuck is your problem, asshole?" he said, grabbing you by the shirt. He shoved you into a stall with his roid rage strength and pushed you to your knees. "You need to cool down," he said, pushing your head toward the toilet with his foot. He flushed, making the water splash onto your face and into your hair. "And quit fucking smoking in school. It's bad for your lungs," he said as he left the bathroom.

The last time you had a bad encounter with Gage was during senior year. You had totally forgotten about an English paper that you had to do. You were in the library and saw him working on it at a computer. "What's that?" you asked.

He looked at you with that look of contempt he always had. "The English paper that's due tomorrow."

"Fuck," you said. "I completely forgot about it."

"Bummer," he said, looking back at the device in front of him.

"I'll give you fifty bucks and/or suck you off if you let me copy yours and change a few things."

He did not even look away from the device, like he couldn't be bothered to give you the time of day. "Sorry, I've been working on this forever."

One of his friends called from across the library. "Dude, coach said you forgot to sign the get-well card for Pete."

"Be right there," he replied, leaving his computer unattended. You glanced over to make sure he wasn't watching you, and you pressed Ctrl-P and printed the document. You ran and got it, changed a few words like you promised, and then passed it off as your own. You didn't think your teacher was even going to read them, but of course she did, and you and he both got called into the office, where he recounted your offer to copy off of him in exchange for sexual favors and accused you of plagiarism. You denied it and tried to explain that he copied off of you, that he was too dumb, and that his comment about you offering to suck him off was homophobic. In the end, both of you had to redo the assignment, and it almost kept you from graduating because it took forever.

Now, almost fifteen years later, you are going to get your revenge for all the times he hurt you. You arrive at Graham's house, hungry for flesh. You try to open his front door, but it's locked. You debate your options and then decide to just knock. He'll open the door, and you'll ambush him. You rap your knuckles against the door and hear. "Just a minute!"

The door opens soon after, and there he is, standing in an A-line shirt and a pair of boxers. He's lost the muscular physique he had in high school and is now paunchy, with a bit of a beer gut. "Hey, dude, long time no see," he says after taking a moment to recognize you. "What brings you here this morning?" You stare at him, about to pounce, when he says, "Whoa, dude, you don't look so good. Come on in. I'll get you a glass of water." You follow him into his home, which is smaller than the one you shared with your husband, and it gives you a bit of joy knowing that you were more successful than him. You glance around the room as Gio goes into the kitchen to get you water. No pictures of family or anything. He's lonely. Probably pushed everyone he knows away with his rotten attitude and general homophobia. "I'm glad we can put our antagonism from high school behind us. I forgive you for all the bullying and shit. I spent my entire high school career closeted. I can't imagine what it was like for you being openly queer. No wonder you were such an asshole bully. It was a defense mechanism."

You grunt, spinning to face him. *You* were an asshole bully? Absolutely the fuck not. He bullied *you*. You take a running start towards the kitchen and tackle him to the ground, spilling the glass of water he was holding all over the floor. You try to scream at him about how he made your childhood a living hell and about how you don't care that he's gay now because he is going to get what he deserves and how you are going to eat his face off and then eat the rest of him, but of course, the only thing that comes out of your mouth is a vicious groaning. You are sitting on his midsection, about to take a bite, when he slides out from underneath you, leaving his boxers behind. You watch as his bare pale ass runs through the kitchen, and you follow. He's going up the stairs two steps at a time, so you take them three at a time, almost catching him at the top, but he ducks into another room and slams the door behind him.

You take a running start and slam through the door, splintering it into a thousand pieces. You're greeted with the barrel of a shotgun. Your first thought should be to try to run and escape, but your real first thought is how ridiculous he looks in a shirt and no bottoms, his little pecker dwarfed by the enormous weapon in his hand.

"You want to know what kind of gay guy I turned out to be? The one who's packing." You duck just in time to avoid a headshot as the gun goes off, but some of the shot hits your shoulder. He cocks the gun again, trying to fire, but the gun is jammed. Instead, he uses it to bludgeon you, knocking you to the floor. He takes off, leaping over you into the hallway, and you pull yourself up to give chase. You're down the stairs and out the door in seconds, watching him running with his ass to the sun. You try to catch him, but he ducks into the woods behind his house. You crash through the branches, looking for him, but can't tell which way he went. The mud on the ground is dry, and both left and right on the trail seem like they've been walked through recently.

If you take a left, go to page 81.

If you take a right, go to page 85.

CHAPTER 19

YOU TAKE A LEFT.

L IS FOR "LEFT." L is for "luck." It's random, but that's your reasoning. You chase through the woods for what could be miles or could also be just a few city blocks. You're not sure. You don't really remember how far these woods stretch. There is no sign of Gordon anywhere. You decide to just keep following the path, hoping it takes you out to the other side of the woods soon.

It's been a few hours, and you are starting to get very hungry, though not necessarily tired. At least being undead is good for your stamina. Suddenly, the trail ends at a cliff. You eye it up, wondering if maybe you could climb it, when you see smoke coming out of a small hole off to the left. Where there's smoke, there's fire, and where there's fire, there's humans. You can eat Gabriel later. You'll eat whatever camper or hermit this is first. You go over to the cave. It's a small opening, but there has to be more space in there with how much smoke is coming out. You crouch down and scoot into the hole, finding that you were correct. It opens into a large cavern. In the middle of the cavern is a bonfire.

“Go away!” you hear a low voice say. You ignore it. You’re starving. “No humans allowed!” Humans? You approach the campfire, peeking behind it to see who is talking to you. It is a large hairy creature, like a cross between a human and an orangutan. You cough. You knew that there had been Bigfoot sightings in these woods before, but you never believed them. Before being resurrected by a cult in some office building basement, you didn’t believe in zombies either, so you guess this isn’t too jarring an encounter. He is almost eight feet tall with coarse red hair covering his entire body. You can make out enormous genitals covered in red bush. His face is kind and almost human, but not enough so that you feel familiarity.

“You’re not human,” the bigfoot says, looking you up and down. “At least not anymore.” You shake your head. “Zombie, right? Been a while since I’ve encountered one. At least two hundred years. Did you know that the Indigenous people had zombies? They didn’t call them that, but they had them. Spirits of the undead. It’s sad, really, what you humans do to others. But I don’t have to tell you that. You look like you’ve been murdered at least once. Have a seat. Let me tell you a story.”

You sit down. You’re hungry, but this is too fascinating to pass up. A real-life cryptid has been living only a mile or two from your home this entire time. You’ve always been fascinated with cryptozoology. You had even considered it as a career until you realized that no sane person actually spent their life searching for Nessie and the mothman.

The bigfoot tells his story. "Millions of years ago, before humans ever came to this continent, my people built civilizations. There were horses in this place, not like the ones you have now, but we tamed them. They pulled our carts and plowed our lands. About a thousand years before humans arrived on this continent, a great plague swept through the land, and many of my people were lost—not just lost, erased, as they had never been here. Their flesh and bones were reduced to mush by a highly contagious sickness with symptoms that were quick and fatal to everyone who contracted it. Eventually, what was left of my people found an antidote to the virus, but it was too late. There were not enough of us left to repopulate, and once the humans arrived over the land bridge, it became impossible. We went into hiding, small families spread throughout the continent, waiting to die out. We have lived for thousands of years. Do you know how long that is? You don't seem like you've been alive, or dead, for very long, have you?"

You shake your head.

"It's forever. I was born before the first Europeans ever arrived on this continent, and I may be the last of my kind. Every once in a while, I hear word of a bigfoot sighting, sometimes thousands of miles away, and I go in search of someone else like me." This story is devastatingly sad, and the way he tells it pulls at your heartstrings. If you could cry, you would.

"It has been over a hundred years since I've encountered another of my kind, and the last time I did, she was very ill and died soon after. It is hard, but I am going to keep looking. I know there has got to be more of us out there. I can't give up hope." Your stomach growls. "I must find companionship." You are so hungry. "I don't want to die having not found love." You are on your feet, leaping towards the bigfoot. You sink your teeth into his neck and tear off a bite of him. It's hairy, so you spit it out.

"Please, stop!" he pleads with you, but you can't stop. You need to eat. You take another bite in the same spot, this time going deeper and getting a mouthful of sinew. You chew as you watch the light drain from the bigfoot's eyes and his blood pool underneath him. The chunk of him in your mouth tastes like nothing. Of course. He isn't human, so he's not edible. Oh well. You'll find someone to eat.

Go to page 89.

CHAPTER 20

YOU TAKE A RIGHT.

YOU'RE RIGHT-HANDED, SO YOU decide that right is the way to go. It's random, but that's your reasoning. You chase through the woods for what could be miles or could also just be a few city blocks. You're not sure. You don't really remember how far these woods stretch. There is no sign of Gideon anywhere. You decide to just keep following the path, hoping it takes you out to the other side of the woods soon.

It's been a few hours, and you are starting to get very hungry, though not necessarily tired. At least being undead is good for your stamina. The path diverges into a clearing where a small cottage sits, smoke billowing from its chimney. Someone lives here. Someone you can eat. The door opens, and you see an old woman, older than Sister David and far more wrinkled. She waves you over, and you go, hungry enough to follow her into the house. "Have a seat, deary," she says. "I'm just about to serve supper."

You sit down without a word, mostly because you can't talk. The house is decorated with various plants and bones. It's certainly not your aesthetic, but the lady has been able to make this décor look chic. "Would you like something to drink?" she asks, and you shake your head. "You must have come a long way to find me all the way out here. I usually don't go into town much. It's a bit of a hike in my old age. Would you believe I'm a hundred and two this week?" You both don't believe it, and you do. She is obviously ancient, but she is also moving around with stunning agility for someone born before the invention of instant coffee.

You take a breath in, and, to your surprise, whatever it is she is cooking smells delicious. This is the first thing you've smelled since you woke up that overpowered the scent of the rotting of your own flesh. The old lady opens her oven, and the scent hits you again, even more powerful and mouthwatering (if your mouth could water anymore. It can't). She brings a small roast to the table and, with a large, scary knife, cuts it open. The meat is juicy and tender, and you can't wait to get a bite. She cuts one half for you and takes the other half for herself. You don't even bother with a fork. You lift the whole piece to your mouth and bite it like you would an apple. It's perfect. Better than that wagyu beef you had in Japan that time your husband took you. The juices dribble down the sides of your mouth, and you wipe them with your hand and lick your fingers, not wanting to waste a drop. You take another bite, and then another, too enamored by the meat to remember that there's only one food that tastes good to you anymore until it's all gone.

"What is this?" you try to say, and, despite it just coming out as a grunt, the old lady figures out what you are asking.

"Why, that's little Jimmy Roberts. It's the last of the meat I have left of him." She brings a bite of her own portion to her mouth. "He wandered into my woods a few months ago and knocked on my door, asking for his mom and dad. I am not his mom and dad, obviously, but I was happy to provide him with some sustenance if he stayed with me for a bit. The poor kid was so hungry, he stuffed himself until he couldn't fit into the cage, the little glutton." She takes another bite and motions to a small dog cage on the floor nearby. "Anyways, at that point, I just had to slaughter and eat him. Kids are so tasty, wouldn't you agree?" She takes the last bite of her portion and then politely wipes her mouth. She then licks the knife that she had used to cut the meat. "Hopefully another little tyke comes along soon." She cackles, and you realize that she's a witch, like the kind from an old fairy tale. You never believed in that shit yourself, but here she is, serving you a dinner of roast kid.

You're horrified. You just ate a piece of a small child. You stand up, ready to give this witch a piece of your mind. Then you remember that you ate your husband not twelve hours ago, so you can't really blame a person for eating what they need to eat. You're also still fucking hungry. You lunge at the old lady, easily taking her down. She opens her mouth and starts chanting something, no doubt a spell, and you clamp your hand over her mouth and then twist her head around, and her neck snaps easier than a pencil. You pick her up and take a bite. Her skin is dry, and you're disappointed as you chew that you cannot taste anything. Do witches not count as human? You decide that once your stomach is finally full, you're going to go to the library and do some research on zombies and what they are and are not allowed to eat. For now, you lick the plate that the witch served her roast on, and then you head out of the cottage.

Go to page 89.

CHAPTER 21

YOU'VE BEEN HIDING UNDER A BRIDGE FOR A WHILE.

You're starving. It's been a week, or maybe longer, but you know that there are probably police looking for you. You'll finish off your enemy list later. For now, you are subsisting on random vagrants who wander under the bridge, usually just the ones that get violent, but sometimes you have to eat one of the less violent ones to make sure you don't starve. The rotting of your flesh has gotten worse, and it's all you can smell now. You can even taste the rotting of your tongue and cheeks.

There is a lady who lives under the bridge who has taken a liking to you. Her name is Irma. She is almost sixty and has a long, sad life story, from some time in the military after 9/11 to various VA mental hospitals due to her PTSD to a home under this bridge. She knows about your hunger, but she doesn't seem to care. She has her own mental health issues going on; she told you the first time she saw you eat a guy. She didn't even look horrified. "Saw a lot of shit in Afghanistan."

She's been trying to teach you to speak to no avail, though your grunts have gotten a bit more articulate as of late, so you've been able to communicate a bit as the two of you go about your day. She's even begun helping you eat, though you're worried because each time you eat a person, the length of time you are satisfied is less and less. Last night, you ate three people, and you were still hungry. The only thing stopping you from eating a fourth was the rising of the sun. You even thought about eating Irma, but you were able to control yourself and went for a walk to stave off the temptation.

You've also begun to decay more. Your flesh is rotting and has gone from the pale green it was to a nasty yellow. The other day, you tried to clean yourself a bit with some accumulated rainwater, but when you pulled off your shoe, one of your toes came with it. You are falling apart.

One early morning, before dawn, Irma wakes you up, excited to show you a potential next meal. You roll over and glance out at someone who is walking under the bridge. He is wearing a hoodie and a pair of khaki pants, and you can't make out much about who he is. It's probably better that way. The less you know about the people you eat, the better. You wait until he's a few feet away from you and quietly leap down from where you have been living the last few days. You slink behind the figure, slowly getting closer to him with every step. You are about to take him down, so close that you can almost taste him, when he turns around and, from his pocket, pulls a small handgun. You don't have time to duck. He's a quick shot. He shoots the gun, and the bullet hits you in the stomach. It's not the first time you've been shot in the last few weeks, and at this point, you're used to it. You try to tackle the man, but he takes off in the other direction. You've had potential meals escape before, and usually let them go, but this motherfucker shot you, so he's going down. You chase after him, but, clear of the bridge, you can't locate him. You look around, trying to figure out where he went. That's when you hear a call from the road that goes over the bridge.

"I'm up here, you undead idiot." You look up at the bridge. He has shucked the jacket he is wearing and stands, armed to the teeth with a vest of knives and guns strapped to his chest over a tan dress shirt. He has a semi-automatic in one hand, and, with the other hand, he places a fedora, the type that only Nazi-hunting archeologists and neckbeard losers wear, onto his head. It's familiar. You think you've seen this guy before. He's well into middle age, and, despite his threatening array of weapons, he's less than intimidating, looking more like an insurance agent than someone who would randomly shoot you.

"I'm Rome Samuel, Zombie Hunter. Prepare to die again." This guy? In the hustle and bustle of dying and being resurrected, you had completely forgotten about him. Never in a million years would you have expected him to show up.

He's got guns, but you are basically bulletproof. "Prepare to die, motherfucker!" you try to say, but it just comes out as a guttural howl. You brace yourself and leap up onto the bridge like the villain in a bad superhero TV show, ready to eat this loser. He lets out a spray of gunfire in your direction, and a few bullets hit you, but they barely slow you down. You take him down at the knees and climb up his body towards his face, hungry for his flesh. Before you're halfway up, he's pulled a machete from his vest, and he swings it at you. You pull away for a second and try to retreat, but he is faster and brings the machete down on your forearm, severing your hand. You howl in shock as you hold the stump of your arm. It doesn't hurt too badly, but it also doesn't feel good.

Leaving your hand on the ground, you retreat under the bridge. Where your hand used to be is just empty space. It's not bleeding because you don't have any blood left in your body, but it's oozing yellow gunk. You decide you'll hide out under the bridge until this zombie hunter is gone, and then you'll go back and retrieve your hand. Irma will be able to help you sew it back on. She was a medic in Afghanistan. Speaking of Irma, she greets you as you approach. "Was he tasty?"

You shake your head, trying to motion for her to hide with some urgency. She's having trouble understanding what you're saying. You hear Rome Samuel's voice taunting you. "You're going back into the grave, you undead fuck!"

"Come on," says Irma. She leads you up into a place where you can hide. It's a tiny little alcove that you can't really see from anywhere under the bridge unless you know where to look. Irma uses it to hide all her belongings, but now, she's hiding you there. "Wait here. I'll distract him."

Irma leaves you to hide and greets Rome. "Howdy, sir, can I help you with anything?" you hear her say. She's got her typical jovial tone, but she's added an extra layer of crazy to try to get the guy to go away.

"Out of my way, lady," he replies. "I know he's here." You can hear Irma trying to distract him, and you stay perfectly still. You hear his footsteps approaching and then a deep sniff. "I can smell him."

"You're not killing anyone!" you hear Irma scream. Then there's a tussle, and you bolt out of your hiding spot to try to help. Irma is a strong lady, but she's had some injuries in her lifetime, both during the war and after, and you don't think she is going to be able to take this guy on her own. You get out of your hiding spot in just enough time to hear a gunshot and watch as Irma's brains are splattered across the side of the bridge. Her body falls to the ground, revealing the grinning face of your assailant.

"NO!!" you shout, and your own voice forming a coherent word shocks you. You lunge at the zombie hunter, but he turns and shoots you as well. It's at close range, and the impact throws you to the ground. Before you can pull yourself up, the man is on top of you, his machete in hand. You try to block him as he raises it, but you only have one hand, and it's pinned underneath you. He brings the blade down on your neck, and you feel your head being severed from your body. You don't die immediately from the loss of your head. Your brain is still operating, though you can feel yourself begin to fade. Your eyes blink slowly as you watch the zombie hunter stand up and walk over to your severed head. He grabs your hair and pulls your head up. The last thought you have is "gosh, buy me a drink first."

If you have massacred the cultists that resurrected you, go to page 95.

If you have not massacred the cultists that resurrected you, go to page 57.

CHAPTER 22

YOU ARE DEAD. FOR REAL THIS TIME.

UNFORTUNATELY FOR YOU, YOU'VE eaten the only people in the city who could have revived you. They were tasty, but in hindsight, it was not really worth eating them if it meant you lost the fountain of eternal life they could have provided you. Your body is taken back to a morgue, but, with your husband a mountain of blood and guts spewed unceremoniously across your bedroom floor, and no one else in your life particularly fond of you, no one comes to claim your body. You're written off as a John Doe and cremated, your whole life and afterlife a baggy full of ashes that are tossed in an unmarked grave. Sucks to be you.

The End.

CHAPTER 23

YOU ARE TOO HUNGRY TO THINK ABOUT WHO IT IS YOU'RE EATING.

You could have used your newfound undeadness for heroic purposes, killing and eating sex traffickers and gang members and the like. Or you could have used it for revenge, eating everyone who has ever wronged you. But you are just too hungry. Even in your ravenous state, you know it's a bad idea for you to eat people in your neighborhood. With the police having found what's left of your husband, they're for sure going to be patrolling the area. You take off in the other direction and tell yourself you're going to go about two miles before you stop to eat someone. You end up only going a mile and a half before you decide you are too hungry to wait.

You turn into a cul-de-sac, and there are three houses, all relatively spaced out. The house in the middle has a for-sale sign in front of it, and the long grass in the large front yard indicates to you that it is long-abandoned. You'll have to go with either the house on the right or the house on the left.

The house on the left is big and white, with a perfectly manicured lawn and flowers planted in various spots across the property. The house itself has to have at least four bedrooms, along with other amenities that make living there a pleasant experience. There are multiple cars in the driveway and a basketball hoop in front of a garage that probably holds more cars. There is a single light on, indicating that at least one person is at home, maybe more, given the number of vehicles on the property. The people in this house clearly care about their property and are good contributors to the neighborhood. However, their big house means money, which means they may be more likely to be missed if you eat them, which could cause problems for you down the road.

The house on the right is smaller and less well-kept. It can't have more than three bedrooms inside, if that. The yard is a mess, overgrown in some places and patchy in others. You see a tennis ball, a lighter, some fast-food wrappers, and a sock spread throughout the yard, along with more things you can't make out. There are no cars parked in the driveway, though a car may be in the garage. No lights are on, so you aren't sure if someone is home or not. The siding on the house is run-down, and you can tell these people don't care about their property. Maybe eating them will be good for the neighborhood. If they're gone, someone else can move in and start taking care of the lawn and fixing things up.

If you decide to go into the house on the left first, go to page 103.

If you decide to go into the house on the right first, go to page 101.

CHAPTER 24

YOU DECIDE TO GO INTO THE HOUSE ON THE RIGHT.

YOU'RE GOING TO DO the neighbors a favor. You creep around the back of the house and check the doorknob. To your delight, it opens. You open the door and slip into the house. You are in a tiny, messy kitchen with piles of dishes in the sink. From the kitchen, you can see into the living room where a filthy couch sits. On top of that couch is a woman in a ratty T-shirt and no pants, snoring loudly. You make your way across the kitchen, but your foot hits something that makes a loud beeping noise, almost like music. You duck off to the side in case it wakes the woman up, and then look to see what you kicked. It's one of those toys with various shapes and letters that talk when you press them. The kind that little kids have. You peek around the doorway to see if you woke the woman up. To your relief, she is still snoring away. You sit down, trying to decide how you're going to do this, when you hear a voice behind you.

"Are you Santa Claus?" You spin around. A little girl has come out of one of the two bedrooms. She is wearing a pink princess shirt that is too big for her, and her hair hangs down to her shoulders.

You bring your finger to your lips to shush her. You shake your head. It's July.

"Are you a policeman?"

You nod, still focused on the woman and your never-ending hunger.

"Are you here to take my momma away?" You think for a second. The answer is, unfortunately, yes. You nod. "If you do that, what's going to happen to me and my brothers and sisters?" Her bottom lip quivers, and tears begin to form in her bright brown eyes.

Brothers and sisters? You glance into the room she came out of. There are two little girls in there on bunk beds. In the other room, two boys sleep on the same small bed. Fuck, you can't eat this woman. No wonder her yard is a mess. She has five kids to take care of, and the oldest isn't even ten years old. You smile at the little girl and make a motion with your thumb, pointing behind you like you're leaving. Her mom's not going anywhere. You put your finger to your lips again like it's a secret that you just broke into her house, and then you leave. The house on the left it is, then.

Go to page 103.

CHAPTER 25

YOU GO TO THE HOUSE ON THE LEFT.

By the number of cars in the driveway, you're going to have a lot of people to eat. You sneak around the back of the house. There's a fence surrounding the backyard, and you scale it easily and drop into the enclosed yard. A pool sits enticingly in the yard, and you touch your hand to it; the water is warm. You decide that after you've eaten everyone inside, you're going to take a dip in the pool. It's been a while since you've been swimming. The city council wouldn't let you and your husband build a pool in your yard. Fuckers. You see a patio door, and you pull on it, excited that it opens easily.

You enter the house, which is cool and air-conditioned. You're in a living room with a massive television against one wall and nice leather furniture against the other. There's no one in this room, but you assume everyone is asleep. It's pretty late at night. You creep through the hallway until you find what you think is a bedroom. You slowly open the door, trying not to make a sound, hoping you'll find someone inside. To your disappointment, it's a home gym, with weight machines and a treadmill, and not a tasty human in sight. You close the door and continue down the hall. The next door is a bathroom with a giant bathtub, bigger than you've ever seen in a home before. After that, there's an empty bedroom that you assume is a guest room. Everyone must be upstairs. You climb the stairs, noticing that they don't creak at all. A real sign of wealth. There are three rooms on the top floor. The first is a bedroom, empty. Then a full bathroom, also empty. Everyone better be in this last room. When you get to the door, you stop, hearing a voice inside the room. It's a man's voice, youngish. He's screaming at someone, presumably on the phone.

"I told you to buy forty shares yesterday!" He pauses, listening to the person on the other side. "I don't care what excuses you have! I told you to buy the stocks, and you didn't, and now I'm screwed, and you're fired." Another pause. "I don't care that you have a wife and kid; you're out of a job. Sign up for unemployment. God! I'm hanging up now. My secretary will send you your letter of termination tomorrow." He hangs up. "Asshole!"

Wow, this guy deserves to be eaten. You burst through the door. When he sees you, the man lets out a high-pitched scream unbecoming of whatever type of businessman he is. He tries to run past you, but you grab him by the back of his white shirt and look at him. He's maybe thirty-five, with short-cropped strawberry-blonde hair and a white dress shirt and slacks. "Put me down!" he shouts, kicking you, but you're holding him at arm's length, and he is short, so he barely grazes you with his kicks. "Do you know who I am?" You don't answer. "That's what I thought!" he screams. "I'm the CEO of Ranger Tech! You've heard of it! I was on the forty under forty list two years in a row." You have heard of Ranger Tech. You try to remember what they do. Oh shoot, they're a weapons manufacturer. You're definitely eating this guy. And you're going to make him suffer.

You set him back down in his chair and push the chair under the desk so he can't escape. You tear his shirt off with one fell swoop, and then you bring his arm to your mouth, taking a bite. He screams bloody murder, but you don't care. The house immediately next door is empty, so it's not like anyone can hear him. You keep eating his arm, slowly, to make him feel more pain. Unfortunately, before his arm is gone, he's dead, so you quickly finish the rest of him off, except his face, which you use to unlock his phone, texting the last person who called that he changed his mind. Then you eat his face, slurping it off his skull. You can taste some expensive moisturizer on the skin as you chew it like taffy.

You're almost satiated, at least for now, but he's still got his brains. You pull his head off and take it down to his kitchen, where you search through his utensil drawers for something you can use to crack his skull open without making a mess of the brains. You find a small ice pick and deftly crack a hole in the top of his skull, then you take it outside, eating the brains like popcorn. Outside, you set the skull down and strip out of your clothes, then you take the skull with you into the pool, where you lounge a bit. The water feels good, and the brains are a nice snack. You float in the pool more easily than you would have floated when you were alive, likely due to the gases being released by your rotting insides. You finish off the last of the brains, and, for a moment, you're not hungry anymore. You are a bit horny. That CEO would have been just your type if you had been alive. You probably would have cheated on your husband with him if you had met him a few weeks ago. You toss his skull onto the concrete near you, smashing it into a thousand pieces. You could spend a little bit of time taking care of yourself right here.

If you masturbate, go to page 107.

If you decide to move on, go to page 109.

CHAPTER 26

HORNY BASTARD. YOU'VE CHOSEN TO SPEND SOME TIME PLEASURING YOURSELF.

You start with your dick. You've always really enjoyed masturbating. It probably kept you from cheating on your husband more often throughout your marriage. Nothing better than spending some time jerking it. You close your eyes and grab your cock with your hand, pumping it, first slowly, then faster. You think first about your husband, then that time you got fucked by a C-list musician after one of his sets that you didn't even want to go to, but your husband did, and then the dude hit you up on an app after. After you're done fantasizing about being fucked by the musician, you think about Brother Thevar and his hot, muscular body. You didn't know cult members could be hot until you met him. After that, your mind wanders to some fucked-up shit. You think about eating this CEO and how it was kind of sexy to watch him bleed out. Then you think about biting off your husband's dick and how satisfying it was. You don't know if getting off to the idea of violence is part of being a zombie, or maybe it was always in you, and you're just unlocking it now.

You stop and look down at your dick. It's not getting hard. Fuck. You finally remember that there's no blood in your system anymore, so you can't become erect. It would have saved you a few minutes if you had thought of that before. At least the back door still works. You put your finger to your asshole and run it around the rim. Then you penetrate it, closing your eyes again. You don't even start with normal stuff this time. Your thoughts just keep going to fucked-up shit. You daydream about eating your first boyfriend from high school, your mom and dad, your mailman, and your neighbor. You think about everyone you've seen since you were raised from the dead, and you wish you had eaten the ones you had not, imagining gulping them down as you ride your fingers. You start to moan. This is working for you. Deep in a fantasy about literally eating your favorite actor's ass, you finally come. You look down at what came out of you. It's tarry and black, like dried blood. The orgasm was nice and needed, but whatever nasty shit this is coming out of you has killed the mood.

Go to page 109.

CHAPTER 27

YOU PULL YOURSELF OUT OF THE POOL.

THEN YOU LEAVE THE backyard, giving the CEO's shattered skull a stomp with your shoe on the way out. That's for all the kids who have been killed with your weapons. You run back upstairs to his room and root through his closet for some leisurewear. Everything is so expensive, but also the dude was kind of short, so it takes you a while to find something that will fit. Eventually, you land on a pair of basketball shorts that probably cost more than your car note, a T-shirt with a logo for a brand you can't afford, the most comfortable boxers you've ever worn, despite them being tight on you, and a jacket. After leaving his house, you walk down the road in the early morning light, trying to figure out what you are going to do next. You can't go back to your old life. The old you is dead (and so is your husband). Maybe you'll start a new life. You know someone who can make you an ID. You feel a twist in your stomach. You had a few fleeting moments of satisfaction, but now you're hungry again. Guess this is what you're doing next.

You are sure that at some point, people are going to wonder where the CEO is and send someone to check on him, so you had better find someone in a different neighborhood. You walk a mile or so, deciding not to run because it is daylight now, and someone might try to stop you to see if you're okay. You pass under a bridge and catch a glimpse of a woman sitting on a flat area near the top of the bridge. You approach her. She is wearing army fatigues and looks to be about fifty-five. She is warming a can of beans over a small fire she's created. "Howdy, stranger. You hungry?" she asks.

You nod. Too hungry. You know this lady isn't hurting anyone, and that eating veterans is probably going to send you straight to hell if you weren't already going there for eating those other people and your generally poor attitude that you've maintained most of your life. You should find someone else to eat, but you can't. You lunge at her and take her down. You decide that killing her immediately would be the most merciful, so you twist her head with a quick motion, snapping her neck. Then you consume her, quickly, not wanting to spend any time relishing the thought of eating this poor woman.

After she has been eaten, you dig through her stuff. You are sure it all smells, but for the last few hours, the only thing you've been able to smell was your own rotten flesh. You could not even smell this lady's blood and guts as you ate her. Nothing in her stuff is usable to you, but for a moment, you feel satisfied. You are not tired, but you close your eyes for a while. You are not sure how long you have had them closed when you feel a gurgling in your stomach. You vomit up the entirety of the homeless woman and the CEO, and then, not wanting to sit around in pools of blood and guts, you take off, hungry again.

You subsist like this for a few days. You rest for the day, and then you go on the prowl at night, eating two or three or sometimes more people each day, and then staying in one of the houses until it is time for you to eat again. You target people who seem to be loners, never eating kids or people who are obviously parents of small children. You may be a zombie, but you're not a monster, at least not that much of one. In almost a week, you've eaten an elderly couple and their in-home nurse, a gay dude who you had hooked up with once on the app a year or so ago who was even tastier the second time, a yoga instructor in her twenties, a bouncer at a local bar who had just gotten home, three construction workers who had been working on the freeway, two more homeless people, and about half a dozen cops. The latter is the easiest to eat. You just stand in an alleyway doing your best to look suspicious, with your hood pulled over your head and your hand in your pockets, and when a police officer comes up to you to ask you what you're doing, you run for about thirty feet, just to get the cop away from the street, and you pounce and eat them quickly. The only thing you have to remember to do is smash their body cam before you leave their skeleton there. Just so the police department can't see who it is who ate their fallen comrade.

The problem is that each time you eat, the length of time you are satisfied is less and less. Last night, you ate three people, and you were still hungry. The only thing stopping you from eating a fourth was the rising of the sun. You've also begun to stink more. Your flesh is rotting and has gone from that pale green that it was to a nasty yellow. You can't smell anything but rotting flesh. The other day, you tried to shower to clean some of the stink off, but when you pulled off your shoe, one of your toes came with it. You are falling apart.

Tonight, you're outside of a red brick house, one you've been staking out for a couple of days. You saw one person go in there once, and it was an older guy, so you know he does not have any young kids. He drives a big asshole truck with hi-risers and very racist bumper stickers. He for sure deserves what's coming to him. It's dark now, and the lights are off, but you saw him get home earlier, so you know he's in there. You slip around back of the house, where you know most people don't lock the door, noticing a path down back into the woods behind the house. A perfect place for you to make your escape when the time comes. You open the door and step into the house. It's dark and surprisingly clean and tidy for a single racist dude who lives alone.

You take a step and hear a weird whirring sound that makes you turn around just in time to jump out of the way of a large knife that has been sent flying in your direction. The knife lodges itself in the wall behind you, and you glance around, trying to figure out who threw it. There's no one there. The house is still empty, but you notice a wire on the ground that you must have tripped over. Who the fuck booby-traps their back door? Is this some kind of paranoid conspiracy redneck? You could seriously lose your head if you're not careful, but then again, you're really, really hungry.

If you decide it's not worth it and you want to go find someone else to eat, go to page 119.

If you want to keep moving through the house, go to page 115.

CHAPTER 28

YOU DECIDE TO KEEP MOVING THROUGH THE HOUSE.

THIS GUY ALREADY DESERVED to be eaten for his racist tiny-penis truck, but now he definitely deserves to be eaten for that crazy-ass booby trap you just barely survived. You slowly make your way through the kitchen and towards the stairs, carefully checking the ground with each step you take to make sure you don't set off any more flying knives. At the bottom of the stairs, you stop and check to make sure that the steps don't have anything that might hurt you. You don't see anything, so you walk up the stairs, making sure to test each step as you go. Your preoccupation with the steps proves to be a major mistake because you do not see the swinging sandbag falling from the top of the stairs until it collides with your head and sends you flying backwards. You crumble to the floor at the bottom, sure that several bones are broken and worried because you know they won't heal. You force your head to turn around to see what happened.

At the top of the stairs is a man, but not the man you have been stalking. This man has a rifle in one hand, and, with the other hand, he places a fedora, the type that only Nazi-hunting archeologists and neckbeard losers wear, on his head. It's familiar. You think you've seen this guy before. He's well into middle age, and, despite his threatening array of weapons, he's less than intimidating.

"I'm Rome Samuel, Zombie Hunter. Prepare to die again." This guy? In the hustle and bustle of dying and being resurrected, you had completely forgotten about him. Never in a million years would you have expected him to show up here. He continues. "Got word of a dirty zombie in the area. People are showing up stripped of their flesh: cops, nurses, and homeless people. You've been a bad corpse. Well, now you've met your match." He cocks his gun and fires at you twice. The bullets hit you, but you don't really feel them. It's not the first time you've been shot; maybe... You can't even remember at this point. Right now, you're more worried about trying to pull yourself to your feet. "I set a trap for you. Do you like it? It was easy enough to find you. Your stench lingers in the air wherever you go. I've been hired to put a stop to your reign of terror, but even if I wasn't making money off of it, I'd still kill you, just for the fun of it."

You manage to get up on one knee, but then your leg collapses out from under you, and you feel the bone shatter into pieces. You look down at your leg. You can see the bones protruding through the skin, and smell the rotten muscles from the inside of your leg.

This is the end. Rome kneels next to you, pulling a machete from his belt. You try to block him as he raises it, but you notice that one of the gunshots so severely damaged your hand that you can't do anything with it. He brings the blade down on your neck, and you feel your head severed from your body. You don't die immediately from the loss of your head. Your brain is still operating, though you can feel yourself beginning to fade. Your eyes blink slowly as you watch the zombie hunter stand up and walk over to your severed head. He kicks it, and the world spins around you as your head rolls through the hallway of this home. Your last thought is "I probably deserved that."

If you have massacred the cultists that resurrected you, go to page 95.

If you have not massacred the cultists that resurrected you, go to page 57.

CHAPTER 29

YOU DECIDE IT'S NOT WORTH IT.

THERE ARE OTHER PEOPLE whose houses are not booby-trapped that you can eat. You turn around to leave, but you don't get more than a few feet from the house when you hear a gunshot and immediately after feel the impact of a bullet hitting you and sending you flying. It hurts, but it's not going to put you out of commission. It's not the first time you've been shot. Or is it? At this point, you don't even remember. You pull yourself to your feet when you are hit a second time. This bullet is closer and knocks you down as well. You look up at your assailant, who is not the man you have been stalking. This man has a rifle in one hand, and, with the other hand, he places a fedora, the type that only Nazi-hunting archeologists and neckbeard losers wear, on his head. It's familiar. You think you've seen this guy before. He's well into middle age, and, despite his threatening array of weapons, he's less than intimidating.

"I'm Rome Samuel, Zombie Hunter. Prepare to die again." This guy? In the hustle and bustle of dying and being resurrected, you had completely forgotten about him. Never in a million years would you have expected him to show up here. He continues. "Got word of a dirty zombie in the area. People showing up stripped of their flesh: cops, nurses, and homeless people. You've been a bad corpse. Well, now you've met your match." He fires again and again, each shot hitting you and keeping you from being able to pull yourself to your feet. "I set a trap for you. Do you like it? It was easy enough to find you. Your stench lingers in the air wherever you go. I've been hired to put a stop to your reign of terror, but even if I wasn't making money off of it, I'd still kill you, just for the fun of it."

Another shot hits you, this one blowing off your foot. You can't stand up now. This is the end. Rome kneels next to you, pulling a machete from his belt. You try to block him as he raises it, but you notice that one of the gunshots so severely damaged your hand that you can't do anything with it. He brings the blade down on your neck, and you feel your head severed from your body. You don't die immediately from the loss of your head. Your brain is still operating, though you can feel yourself beginning to fade. Your eyes blink slowly as you watch the zombie hunter stand up and walk over to your severed head. He kicks it, and the world spins around you as your head rolls down the hill behind the house. Your last thought is "I probably deserved that."

If you have massacred the cultists that resurrected you, go to page 95.

If you have not massacred the cultists that resurrected you, go to page 57.

CHAPTER 30

YOU'RE ALREADY DEAD. YOU MIGHT AS WELL MAKE THE MOST OF IT.

YOU'RE GOING TO EAT people who deserve it, like Dexter, but for zombies. You're going to be a goddamn superhero with your speed and strength and ability to consume a person in less than fifteen minutes. Do they have zombie superheroes? You aren't sure, but you'll be the first if they don't. Now, what villains are you going to eat?

You walk down the streets of your city, looking for a criminal to consume. You don't have to go far. On the corner, a young woman is being accosted by a man. By the way she's dressed, she's a prostitute. She's small and thin, with long dark hair. She's wearing a tight blue dress and has a lot of makeup on. The man is tall and handsome and wearing a suit, but he's also grabbing her by the hair and pulling on her clothes, so you don't take any time to ogle him, instead running towards the pair. You grab the man and pull him off the woman. "Thank you!" she says, exasperated. "This guy's been harassing me. I told him I was done for the night, but he's been trying to get me to fuck him."

"Come on, Candi," the other man pleads. "You've done it before. You know it goes quick."

"Yeah, too quick. I said no, David."

"That's not even my name," he replies. "My name is Steve."

"And my name's not fucking Candi, but I'm not fucking sleeping with you."

You are holding the man by the neck of his suit, and he slips out of it and runs at not-Candi, grabbing her again. If there was ever someone who needed to be eaten, it's this guy. You run to him and tackle him to the ground. You can smell his nasty cologne. It's even overpowering the smell of your rotting flesh. Before you've stopped tumbling, you've taken a bite out of his neck. He screams, and not-Candi says, "Don't hurt him!"

Oops, too late. You look up at her, his blood running down your face. You chew on his flesh that tastes too much like the cologne. You spit it out. Not-Candi screams and runs off, calling for the police for help. You'll need to eat this guy fast before she sends the cops after you. You throw David/Steve over your shoulders and carry him to an alleyway, where you strip him of his suit, pocketing his wallet in case you need money later. The man is covered in hair and has a relatively small dick, though you'd still have sucked him off if he were alive and wanted you to. Technically, you are still going to suck it, though sucking a dick down your throat is not quite the same as blowing someone. You try to take a bite of his arm, but that's covered in cologne, too. Every inch of his body is covered in cologne. You see some rainwater that's accumulated in a discarded bucket nearby, and you dip the dead man's boxers in it and use them to wipe his skin down. It's a bit better now, but he still doesn't taste good. Not like your husband, who had been freshly showered when you ate him.

You're down to just one of his hairy legs when you hear a voice coming down the alley.

"Crazy fucking prostitute. Why are we even checking this out?"

"Because she was hot."

"Come on, I was going to get a donut. No one is out here eating random johns. This isn't Wisconsin."

A pair of cops is coming down the alleyway, both overweight with big, bushy mustaches, like most of the officers in this city. You glance around, looking for a place to hide. There's a dumpster, but it might be hard to hide there. You look down at the ground where you stand. There's too much blood and guts for you to hide. Dammit, David/Steve, why did you have to go and make a mess? You could eat these cops, but you're supposed to be a hero. Then again, cops are kind of bad guys, aren't they? Would you be a worse person for letting them go or for eating them? These especially seem a bit evil, but then again, you don't have any confirmation that they have done anything except talk shit about not-Candi.

If you are the kind of superhero who eats asshole cops, go to page 127.

If you are not the kind of superhero who eats asshole cops, go to page 143.

CHAPTER 31

YOU ARE THE KIND OF SUPERHERO WHO EATS ASSHOLE COPS.

You leave the john's leg in the middle of the street as a trap and then hide behind a dumpster nearby. You hear one of the cops scream, "What the fuck!" You peek out and see both cops looking at the severed leg. One of them sees the rest of the john's discarded bones and walks over to them. He's within reach of you, and you grab him by the neck and quickly pull him back, pulverizing his head against the brick building behind you.

"Smith?" the other cop calls. He sees Smith's legs peeking out from behind the dumpster and runs to them, his gun ready. He doesn't get a chance to use it. You are on him in milliseconds, and you tackle him to the ground. You put one foot on his neck and grab his head, pulling on it. He screams, and his eyes bulge as you pull with all your might on his skull. You hear a sickening tearing of flesh, and you smile as his head is ripped from his body, taking his spine along with it. Some blood spurts out of his mouth, and you use your tongue to lap it off his pretty face. In the morning light, you eat him first. You reach into the bloody hole of his neck and pull out his intestines like a child grabbing popcorn out of a popcorn bucket at the movies. Then you strip him to his bones and move on to the other cop, eating him to the bone too. You're about to finish off the last of the john when you hear a scream come from above you. You look up, seeing a woman standing on her fire escape with a handful of wet laundry. She shrieks again.

"Help! Police!" You take off running in the direction that you came down the alleyway. Thankfully, no police answer her call, probably because the ones that were patrolling nearby have been eaten. You keep running until you find another alleyway you can duck into. There, you stop to catch your breath. You only have a moment before your stomach gurgles in the same way it did after you ate Matt. You quickly run to a dumpster and open it, hurling your guts into the receptacle. You don't get a chance to look in the dumpster before you vomit the two police officers and the john through your mouth and nose into it, but after you've stopped puking and have cleared the blood and guts from your nostrils, you notice two smells. The first is an overpowering smell of rotten flesh, not coming from you, but coming from the dumpster that you just vomited into. The police officers' guts still smell fresh, so that's not it. Maybe you're behind a restaurant that just threw out a bunch of meat. The second smell that hits you almost overpowers the first. It's the smell of roasting meat, the best you've ever smelled. It's like that first steak at the beginning of spring, when you're able to break out the grill for the first time that year. There's a hint of barbecue sauce in the air, but mostly, you're just smelling the delicious meat. You decide to follow it, though you are covered in blood. You deposit the jacket you're wearing, now ruined, into the garbage, leaving you in a T-shirt. You take some accumulated rainwater and use it to clean the blood and guts off of your face, hands, and hair. You go down the alleyway, following your nose, and emerge in front of a butcher shop. That must be where the delicious smell is coming from, and also why the back of the alley stinks of rotten flesh. You enter the store.

The inside of the butcher shop has two sides. The right side is where the meat is butchered. There are pristine white walls and a small waiting area, and rows and rows of raw meat: ground beef, sausages, steaks of all cuts and sizes, whole chickens, and no-longer-whole chickens. You don't care about that part. The left side of the store is the important side. It is a tiny café with a menu overhead and plenty of seating. There is only one other customer there, eating a French dip sandwich and drinking a soda. You walk up to the counter, hungry again and wanting to taste the meat that you smell.

"How can I help you?" asks the woman at the counter. She is maybe fifty with dark hair and no makeup. She is sturdily built, not overweight, but muscular and stocky. You open your mouth to speak, and then you remember that you can't. It's one of the many things you can't do as a zombie. You make a motion at your mouth, trying to indicate that you are mute. She understands and grabs a piece of paper and a pencil and hands them to you.

You haven't written since you were resurrected, and, for a moment, you're worried that you won't be able to make intelligible letters. But it's easy enough, if a little shaky. You write, "Whatever that smell is. I want that."

She looks at the paper and smiles. "That is our prime cut. Very expensive. Thirty-five dollars for a sandwich. We have cheaper options too if you'd like that." You shake your head and reach into your pocket, pulling out a hundred-dollar bill you took from one of your David/Steve "You want the expensive cut?" You nod, holding up two fingers. "Damn, two?" You nod again. "You must be really hungry. Coming right up." She hands you your change, and you sit down at the table. Less than ten minutes later, the lady brings out two sandwiches. They are piled high with shredded meat between two slices of golden toast. Next to the sandwiches are various veggies and condiments. You don't even bother putting them on. You just grab a piece of the meat and put it in your mouth. It's like heaven. It melts on your tongue, greasy and delicious. You try to place the animal it came from. Venison, maybe? You swallow it and then lift the whole sandwich and take a bite, but the bread tastes like sandpaper on your tongue. You spit it out, suddenly remembering you can't eat human food anymore. Only food that is made out of humans. Then why does this meat taste so good? It all comes together: the obscenely high price, the smell of rotting flesh in the dumpster—this didn't come from an animal. It came from a human being. You nonchalantly get the lady at the counter's attention and motion for the door like you'll be right back.

"Want me to look after your food?" she asks. "You paid a lot for it." You nod and then run out the door, going back into the alleyway. You open the dumpster back up, looking for confirmation of your suspicions. You dig through piles of police officers and john meat until you find what you are looking for: a human foot. Certainly not one that you ate. You would have eaten this down to the bone. This diner is selling human meat. And you're sure they're not ethically sourcing it like you have been for at least the last eight hours. You're a zombie superhero now. You have to put a stop to this cannibal diner.

You return to the diner and wave a thank-you to the lady at the counter, sitting back down at your table. You decide it would be worse for you to let this meat go to waste than to eat it, so you devour the rest of the meat while you contemplate your next steps. You could go back there right now and kill everyone who works here, saving anyone else who might be butchered today. Or you could stake out the place and kill the workers at night. They might not do their butchering during the day. It might attract attention. Plus, killing them at night will give you a better opportunity to shut down this entire operation.

If you go back there right now to put a stop to the butchering, go to page 133.

If you decide to stake out the place, go to page 139.

CHAPTER 32

YOU DECIDE TO GO BACK THERE RIGHT NOW AND PUT A STOP TO THIS BUTCHERING.

You can't risk anyone else being butchered in the next few hours. You finish your sandwiches and head out the door, heading straight back into the alleyway You saw a back door while investigating. It's probably better to go in through that way to avoid having someone alert the police.

You're in luck. Someone is coming out the back door with a garbage bag. It's a younger man with a porn stache and bulging eyes, wearing a white apron covered in blood. The man opens up the dumpster and hoists the garbage bag into it. Then he opens the door to the restaurant again. You use this opportunity, racing towards him and slamming him into the door. He falls to the ground, his head hitting the door frame with a crack, and he lies in the corner of the frame. You slam the door shut on his face, denting it in. You'll eat him later.

You enter the building. To your right, you see a kitchen, and, to your left, you see a basement. It's probably better to start in the basement and lure some of the other employees down so you don't cause a ruckus near the dining room. You go down the dingy steps that open into a dark basement. The floor is a layer of dirt and muck, and the walls are covered in dried blood. Up ahead of you, you see a rack with four hooks. Dangling from three of those hooks are the dead, naked bodies that are going to be turned into sandwiches. The first is a heavyset woman who has already been filleted. Various pieces are missing from her body, including most of the left side of her torso, exposing her rib bones and some of her organs. Next to her is an older man; you can tell by the wrinkles on his body, but you can't guess an exact age because there is no head. Instead, his bloody stump of a neck stares at you. A couple of weeks ago, you would have been disgusted by seeing a severed neck, but you've seen worse in the last twenty-four hours. You've done worse. Finally, there is a young blond man about your age. He's still in perfect condition except for a metal pipe sticking out of his neck, from which blood is running into a bucket on the floor. He must be fresh. A sulfurous smell fills the air, and you realize his body is expelling its waste, which begins to drip down his leg. You look away in disgust and see a door off to the side. From the door, you hear a muffled, panicked screaming.

You run to the door and realize your delay in looking at those bodies has cost you. There is a young man tied up naked on the table with a sock or something in his mouth. Standing over him is a man in black clothing and a white apron, a mask covering his face. Before you can get close enough to stop him, the man in the apron puts a pike on the young victim's temple and slams a hammer that is in his other hand onto the pike, driving it into the young man's head. Some superhero you are. It's not too late for the killer to die, though, so you pounce on him. You could eat him alive, but you are worried that if you start eating, you are not going to be able to stop, and there are still more people in this restaurant who need to be eaten. You grab the hammer from the man's hand and slam it into his forehead. His skull shatters into a thousand pieces, and his brains join the muck and viscera of his victims on the floor.

"What's going on down there?" asks a voice at the top of the stairs. "Don't tell me another one escaped, Davey. Hang on, I'm coming down with the shotgun." You hide at the doorway, waiting for whoever it is to round the corner. He's a chef, and, though he makes a mean sandwich, you are going to kill him. You tackle him to the ground as he comes into view, kicking his shotgun out of his reach. You decide you're going to be clever about this one. You drag him, still alive and kicking, back into the room with the meat hooks. You take him to the empty one, which was reserved for the now-dead young man in the other room, and you lift him by the front of his shirt until the back of his neck aligns with the meat hook, then you pull him down onto it. With a thud, the hook goes through his brainstem and protrudes out of his eyeball, splattering you with gore. You lick the blood off the end of the hook. Now it's time for the woman upstairs.

You come back up the stairs into the kitchen, where various foods are being prepared. By the smell of it, you can tell that some of the meat is human and some of the meat is from animals. That must have been the cheaper shit. You see a bell that is meant to indicate when an order is ready, and you press it a few times.

"Hang on, Freddy," the woman says, then she turns around, and you duck out of sight. "Freddy? Where'd you go? Where's my order?" She sighs and then enters the kitchen. You grab a large butcher knife from the counter and run at her. See how she likes being butchered. She is defenseless and, shockingly, a bit slow. You would have thought someone who sells human meat for a living would know how to hold her own, but she doesn't block a single blow. You lodge the knife in her neck and watch as the light fades from her eyes. As she falls to the floor, you look into the lobby, which is now empty, then run to the door and change the "open" sign to "closed." It's time for you to feast.

You go back to the kitchen, trying to decide who you are going to eat first, when you hear the ringing of a bell at the door. Fuck. Can't they see that you're closed? They're closed. It's not like you're going to keep this business running after you've eaten most of the staff. Your mind races, trying to decide how you're going to shoo away this customer. You could always eat them. They are here at the shop for human meat after all, though you can't be sure that they actually know what's going on here, and you're supposed to be a hero, so you probably won't eat him if you can help it. You look out at the lobby to see who it is that came in. It's a man, maybe fifty, wearing a safari outfit and a fedora, the type that only Nazi-hunting archeologists and neckbeard losers wear. It looks familiar.

"'Scuse me," the man says. "Has anyone seen a zombie around here? I saw evidence of one outside." This guy? In the hustle and bustle of dying and being resurrected, you had completely forgotten about him. Never in a million years would you have expected him to show up here. You make eye contact with him by accident, and he immediately clocks you for what you are. A zombie. "My name is Rome Samuels," he says. "Prepare to die again." You run to the back door and try to push it open, but it won't budge. You look out the window to see that someone has pushed the dumpster in front of the door. "I figured you would be in here, so I took the liberty of blocking the exits. It's just you and me now."

You run down the stairs. There are plenty of weapons you can use to fight him down there. At the bottom of the stairs, you grab Freddy's shotgun and hide behind the row of dead bodies, peeking through the legs of one of the corpses as Rome comes down the stairs. "Is this your perverted hideout? All these victims. You won't take another!"

You understand why he might think that. The optics are not great, and you can't really explain to him that you're a superhero zombie, only eating people who deserve it. You leap out from behind the row of corpses and fire at Rome, missing. You've never fired a gun before, but he has. He shoots twice, hitting you both times in the knees, blowing your legs out from under you. You fall on your face. This is not the first time you've been shot. Or is it? You can't even remember. You're only focused on escaping or overpowering this guy. He grabs one of the large knives from the table. "This is the end for you, zombie," he says as he raises the knife over his head. You try to block him, but he just swings the blade, cutting off your hand. Damn, that knife is sharp. He steps on your chest and then brings the blade down on your neck, and you feel your head severed from your body. You don't die immediately from the loss of your head. Your brain is still operating, though you can feel yourself begin to fade. Your eyes blink slowly as you watch the zombie hunter stand up and walk over to your severed head. He kicks it, and the world spins around you as your head rolls across the floor of this mucky restaurant basement. Your last thought is "At least I died a hero."

If you have massacred the cultists that resurrected you, go to page 95.

If you have not massacred the cultists that resurrected you, go to page 57.

CHAPTER 33

YOU DECIDE TO STAKE OUT THE PLACE.

THEY PROBABLY AREN'T DOING any butchering during the day. This will give you more time to make a plan, and if you kill the staff at night, you'll have more time to eat them and then leave some notes for the police about what is happening in this building. You finish your sandwiches and then leave the building. You see a rooftop across the street that will be perfect for watching the comings and goings of the business. Your first zombie superhero stakeout! You leap from fire escape to fire escape like a bad supernatural teen show villain and then park yourself directly across from the building.

It's a few hours later, and you've decided you've underestimated the patience you have for stakeouts. Next time, you're just rushing in. Then you see the woman from the store change the "open" sign to "closed." Now is your chance. You climb back down from the fire escape and run across the street. You watch as the back door of the restaurant opens and the lady walks out. As she leaves, you tackle her back through the doorway. Right inside the door is a staircase going down to the basement, and the woman is unable to brace herself. She falls down the stairs, and you watch as her head bounces against the wall and then a series of steps. You follow her to the bottom of the stairs and look at her mangled body. That was easy enough. You glance around the dingy basement. The floor is a layer of dirt and muck, and the walls are covered in dried blood. Up ahead of you, you see a rack with four hooks. Dangling from those hooks are the dead, naked bodies that are going to be turned into sandwiches. The first is a heavyset woman who has already been filleted. Various pieces are missing from her body, including both sides of her torso, which exposes her rib bones and some of her organs. The rest of them are missing. She's already been picked through. Next to her is an older man; you can tell by the wrinkles on his body, but you can't guess an exact age because there is no head. There are also no arms or legs. The third is a young blond man about your age. He's in good condition, though his body is blue. He must be tomorrow's meat. The fourth is a fit man who is a few years younger than you. He is in perfect condition except for a metal pipe sticking out of his neck, from which blood is running into a bucket on the floor. A sulfurous smell fills the air, and you realize his body is expelling its waste, which begins to drip down his leg. He must have just been killed. Fuck! Some zombie superhero you are, letting innocent citizens die like this. You'll avenge him by eating this woman and then burning this place to the ground.

You return to the dead employee's body and kneel, ready to eat, when you hear the door at the top of the stairs begin to open. Fuck. You should have locked it. It's probably one of the other employees returning to get their keys or something. You look up at the intruder. It's a man, maybe fifty, wearing a safari outfit and a fedora, the type that only Nazi-hunting archeologists and neckbeard losers wear. It looks familiar.

"My name is Rome Samuels," he says. "Prepare to die again." This guy? In the hustle and bustle of dying and being resurrected, you had completely forgotten about him. Never in a million years would you have expected him to show up here. He points a gun down the stairs, and you duck away. You glance around the room, trying to find something you can use as a weapon. There's a big knife nearby, and you grab it, but you wish you had a gun or something.

When Rome Samuels reaches the bottom of the stairs, he gasps. "In all my years of zombie hunting, I've never seen an operation quite like this. Are there other zombies working for you? Oh, wait, you can't answer. Regardless, I'm gonna kill you and every zombie in this entire town." You take the knife and run towards him, but he's quicker than you. He shoots you in the chest, and you fly backwards, dropping your knife. You're still alive (or undead) despite the bullet wound to your chest that you are sure you can stick your hand through. This isn't the first time you've been shot. Or maybe it is. You can't remember anymore. Rome picks up your knife and steps towards you. You pull yourself to your feet and charge at him, but he stabs you in the neck and then shoots you again. You fall to the ground once more. This is the end. He takes hold of the knife and pulls it across your neck, sawing as he goes. You feel your head severed from your body. You don't die immediately from the loss of your head. Your brain is still operating, though you can feel yourself begin to fade. Your eyes blink slowly as you watch the zombie hunter stand up and walk over to your severed head. He kicks it, and the world spins around you as your head rolls across the floor of the restaurant's basement. Your last thought is "At least I died a hero."

If you have massacred the cultists that resurrected you, go to page 95.

If you have not massacred the cultists that resurrected you, go to page 57.

CHAPTER 34

ALL COPS ARE BASTARDS, BUT YOU'RE NOT GOING TO EAT THESE ONES.

Guess you're not that kind of superhero. These guys are assholes, but you're going to save the eating for legitimately awful people. You take off in the opposite direction from the cops, tossing your now-bloody hoodie onto the ground as you run. Behind you, you hear one of the cops scream, "What the fuck!" But you are too far away for them to do anything about it.

You've gone a few blocks, and you decide that you've probably lost them. If they run your DNA or whatever, they're just going to come back with the DNA of someone who is for sure dead. Let them try to figure that one out. It's early morning now, and you're walking the streets when you feel a gurgle in your stomach, the same one that you felt after you ate Matt. Time to clear the dead john from your system.

You're in a residential neighborhood, and it must be trash day because everyone has their dumpsters out on the curb. That's convenient. You open the nearest can and vomit into it, the dead john pouring from your nose and mouth. When you're done vomiting, you hear shrieks coming from nearby. Crap, someone saw you. You glance around, trying to place the screams. There's a woman nearby, but she's not facing you. She's facing in the other direction, screaming after a white, windowless van that is driving away. "My daughter!"

This is your chance to do some good. You take off after the van, running at your top speed. You surprise yourself that you're able to catch up to the back of the vehicle. You grab onto the back door handle and pull it open, revealing who is inside. There are two men in the back, holding a young girl tightly by the arms. You push yourself a bit harder and jump into the van.

Up close, you can see what you're dealing with. There are two muscular guys in the van, both a few years older than you, with shaved heads and tattoos. The little girl, maybe about eight years old, is between them, crying. She has long dark hair and is wearing princess pajamas.

A third guy that you can't really see is driving the van. One of the men in the back pulls out a gun, but you easily disarm him. Then you grab the man's head. You think about twisting it off, but you don't want to traumatize the little girl more than she already is. Instead, you use the man's head to knock out the other guy, slamming both of them together. You grab onto the little girl and watch as the unconscious men fly out of the car and skid against the pavement. Now it's time to take out the driver. You pull yourself into the passenger seat, and the man who is driving screams. He's younger than the other guys and really thin. *Not a lot of meat on him*, you think. You grab onto the steering wheel, pulling it to the side, and the man tries to fight you.

"Get off of me!" he yells as you struggle with the steering wheel. Neither of you is watching where the vehicle is going until it is too late. The van collides with a telephone pole, and you and the driver try to brace yourselves, but since neither of you is wearing a seatbelt, you both fly through the front window. You hit the ground, and it hurts, but not as much as you thought it would hurt being thrown through a car window. Good thing you're already dead. The other guy isn't so lucky. You watch as his body skids across the pavement, his face being torn to shreds. By the time he stops, there's nothing left except a sheet of raw bone, flesh, and a single eyeball hanging out of his eye socket by a long, stringy, pink nerve. You pick the eyeball up and pull, tearing it from the nerve like you're picking a piece of fruit from a tree, and put it in your mouth, feeling it roll around on your tongue like a gumball. Then you bite down, feeling it pop and tasting the sweet juices as they fill your mouth. You look down at the man. He's still breathing. Good. He's going to die here, but at least it won't be quick. You check yourself for damage. Your ribs hurt, and your head hurts a little bit, but you're starting to feel better already, and you don't think anything is broken.

Shit, the girl. You run back to the vehicle to check on her. Thankfully, she's fine. A bit bruised and with a small cut on her arm from some broken glass, but she'll live. The trauma of being abducted is probably going to be worse for her in the long run than going through a car crash. You pick her up and walk back towards her mom. The little girl is not speaking, but she hugs you tight, ignoring the scent of rotting flesh emanating from your body. It feels good to be a hero.

You crest the hill towards the little girl's home and see her mom. She's hot, and you don't even like women. She's tall and fit, with long dark hair and light brown skin. Even after crying for the last fifteen minutes, her facial features are stunning. She's got a nose ring and is wearing a crop top that hugs her full frame. She sees you and runs to you, screaming. The police are already there, and she has been talking to them. Shoot. You'll have to run before they want to talk to you too. "Estefania!"

"Mami!" It's the first time you've heard the girl talk.

"Thank you so much," the mom says to you, and you nod, trying to indicate a "you're welcome."

She seems to understand. "They said some trafficking ring has been taking little girls. I thought for sure I was never going to see her again. So many kids are missing from our neighborhood. I thought Estefania was going to be another one of those posters. Thank you so much!"

You nod again and hand Estefania off to her mom. Then, as a police officer calls to you, you run away. You're hungry, but you can't go back to the traffickers now. The police will want to take any live ones into custody, and you wouldn't want to get in the way of the investigation.

After a few blocks of running, you've lost anyone chasing you. The pain from the accident has almost subsided, and you're back at your full strength. Ahead of you, you notice the side wall of a gas station that's covered in paper. You haven't seen that before, and you used to drive past here all the time when you were alive. You get closer to see what it is. They're 'missing' posters. Dozens of posters of missing boys and girls, about the same age as Estefania. Some of them date back about a month, some are brand new. The trafficking ring. This is going to be your arch nemesis. You are going to save these kids.

If all of these kids have been abducted in the last month, you doubt that the people you took out earlier were working alone. There's a park nearby. One that a lot of kids play at. You decide that you're going to stake it out, but first, you need something to eat. You're starving, and that eyeball earlier was not filling enough. There's got to be a bad guy around here somewhere that you can eat.

As if by divine intervention, you hear your next meal screaming nearby. "You fucking bitch, I'm going to kill you!" It's a woman's voice, and it's coming from a house two doors down from the gas station.

A different woman says, "Please, Angelica, leave me alone."

"You're in my house! You leave *me* alone!"

Then you hear the sound of skin hitting skin. A minute or two later, the front door opens, and a small butch woman in cargo pants and a T-shirt leaves the house. She has a red mark on her cheek. "Please just cool down, Angelica," she calls back into the house. "I'll be back in a few hours. I'm gonna get something to eat." She gets on a motorcycle and takes off.

Angelica shouts after her. "Fuck you! I hope you choke on it and die, you fucking cunt!" You decide that eating a domestic abuser is superhero behavior, so you wait until the coast is clear and then run up to the door. It's open, and you enter.

"What the fuck!" the woman inside calls. She's much taller than her partner, with long hair and a septum piercing. You can't explain to her why you're going to eat her, but you hope that the consumption happening immediately after she slapped the shit out of her girlfriend demonstrates to her that it's karma. You grab her by the back of the shirt and drag her through the house, looking for a bathroom. Her partner is going to be traumatized enough walking in on her girlfriend's skeleton, so you don't want her entire nicely decorated living room to be ruined as well.

You drag Angelica into the bathroom as she screams for help. You'll have to be quick. If you could hear her being violent two doors down, then probably the whole neighborhood can hear her being eaten now. In the bathroom, you pull up her shirt and take a bite of her pale, exposed torso. She screams again, and you shut her up by slamming her head into the edge of the toilet. Then you dismantle her, eating quickly. You give yourself five minutes, eating just enough to give you the energy to try to find this trafficking ring. Then you grab one of her jackets, which is a bit tight but overall okay, as well as a copy of a book that is sitting on her counter to occupy your time while you stake out the park. You leave through the back door so as not to attract any attention from the neighbors

You get to the park that you're going to stake out to try to catch the trafficking ring. Your first superhero stakeout. You look for a place to hide and watch. You could always sit on the bench and read a bit while keeping an eye out for creeps, though you may be mistaken for a creep yourself if you do that. Or you could hide in the bushes nearby, though that might make it difficult for you to get to the kids in time if they are abducted quickly.

If you hide in the bushes, go to page 151.

If you sit on the bench and read, go to page 155.

CHAPTER 35

YOU DECIDE TO HIDE IN THE BUSHES.

It's less conspicuous that way. Plus, any traffickers are going to be more likely to abduct a child if there aren't grown men around. You look both ways to make sure no one is watching you, then you duck into the bushes near the park. The playground is big as far as playgrounds go, with several slides, monkey bars, and various climbing poles. Everything is painted a deep, pleasing blue. There are a few kids on the playground and a couple of moms watching them. Now it's time to wait. You watch the playground intently, scanning for potential predators for several hours. You don't get tired anymore, not since you died, so you don't have to worry about falling asleep.

You have been watching the playground for an hour or two, and it's cleared out except for one little girl, her mom, and the mom's dog. The little girl is playing in a sandbox when the dog suddenly starts barking and taking off in the other direction. The leash that the mom had been using to control her pet slips out of her hand, and she runs after it. At that moment, a nearby car door opens, and you see a man leave the vehicle and start running towards the girl. You try to run, but something wraps around your neck and prevents you from doing so. You bring your hands to your throat to try to figure out what it is. Some kind of wire. You turn around to see a man holding a stick attached to the wire around your neck. It's some kind of contraption that might be used to capture a wild animal. The man holding it is about fifty years old, wearing a safari outfit and a fedora, the type that only Nazi-hunting archeologists and neckbeard losers wear. It looks familiar.

"My name is Rome Samuels," he says. "Prepare to die again." This guy? In the hustle and bustle of dying and being resurrected, you had completely forgotten about him. Never in a million years would you have expected him to show up here. You try to motion to the little girl, trying to explain to him that the little girl is more important, but he just tightens the wire around your neck. You can feel it cutting into your flesh.

"I smelled you out here. After that surveillance footage of you eating that eyeball, I knew exactly what I was dealing with. Filthy undead scum. He pulls a machete from his belt and pulls you closer to him. You try to block the first swing of the blade with your hand, but it lops your hand right off. He raises the machete.

"The girl!" you say, shocked by the clarity of the voice coming out of your mouth. He doesn't heed your warning, swinging the blade at you. You feel your head severed from your body. You don't die immediately from the loss of your head. Your brain is still operating, though you can feel yourself beginning to fade. Your eyes blink slowly as you watch the zombie hunter notice the commotion of the little girl being abducted. Your last thought is "Please be as good at saving little girls as you are at hunting zombies."

If you have massacred the cultists that resurrected you, go to page 95.

If you have not massacred the cultists that resurrected you, go to page 57.

CHAPTER 36

YOU DECIDE TO SIT ON THE BENCH.

It's going to provide you with a better vantage point. The playground is big as far as playgrounds go, with several slides, monkey bars, and various climbing poles. Everything is painted a deep, pleasing blue. There are a few kids on the playground and a couple of moms watching them. Now it's time to wait. You watch the playground intently, scanning for potential predators for several hours, pretending to read the copy of *Stone Butch Blues* you stole from Angelica. You don't get tired anymore, not since you died, so you don't have to worry about falling asleep.

You have been watching the playground for an hour or two, and it's cleared out except for one little girl, her mom, and the mom's dog. The little girl is playing in a sandbox when the dog suddenly starts barking and taking off in the other direction. The leash that the mom had been using to control her pet slips out of her hand, and she runs after it. At that moment, a nearby car door opens, and you see a man leave the vehicle and start running towards the girl. You start to stand up to stop him, but you decide that following him will be a better idea. You can kill a lot more human traffickers that way, and you'll be able to eat them in private instead of trying in public to get a few bites in. From your adventure earlier, you know you can keep up with a car, and so, as the man throws the little girl in the trunk of the car and drives off, you follow. It's only a few blocks away that the car comes to a stop, and the man exits the vehicle, opens the trunk, and takes the little girl inside while you watch from around the corner. It's now or never. You follow the man into the building.

The place is horrifying. There are rows of dog crates on the ground, each one occupied with a small child. You quickly count them, realizing that not every child who was on a missing persons poster is also here. You hope they're just in some other warehouse, because it's better than the alternative. Some of these children are extremely malnourished, and most of their clothes are disgusting. Most of them are sleeping or worse, but there are a couple awake and shivering in fear. The guy who brought the little girl in has taken her to an empty cage. She's wailing, and he's berating her. "Quit your crying. Three of my friends died today, and you don't see me crying like this."

You scan the room for other traffickers, not seeing any. The man throws the girl in the cage and slams the door, roughly enough that you want to kill him right now. You rush to him, grabbing him by the shirt collar. "What the fuck! Who are you?"

You don't answer. You can't answer, but even if you could, you wouldn't. You drag him out of eyeshot of the kids, and you throw him to the ground forcefully. Then you stomp on his skull until there's no skull left. Fucking sex-trafficking pervert. "Chris?" you hear a voice from nearby and then a toilet flush. Shit, there's another one. You see the door open, and you rush to meet it. A chubby guy is coming out of the bathroom, but you push him back in. The bathroom is disgusting. A fitting place for this guy to die.

"Who are you?" the guy asks, but you just spin him around so his face is on the toilet. You stick your finger in his mouth and pry his teeth open, placing them around the edge of the toilet bowl. Then you use your foot to shatter his teeth and the rest of his skull against the porcelain. You pick up a piece of his skull and lick the brain and blood out, trying to figure out how you'll get these kids medical attention without being able to communicate. You're also hungry, so you'll have to eat these guys before you begin any rescue operation. The kids will survive for an hour while you chow down, right? From outside, you hear the kids calling and screaming, but there's also another voice.

"I know you're in there, you sick, sex-trafficking zombie!" What the fuck? You open the bathroom door and look out to see a man of about fifty years old, wearing a safari outfit and a fedora, the type that only Nazi-hunting archeologists and neckbeard losers wear. It looks familiar.

"My name is Rome Samuels," he says. "Prepare to die again." This guy? In the hustle and bustle of dying and being resurrected, you had completely forgotten about him. Never in a million years would you have expected him to show up here. You shut the bathroom door, hoping to give yourself some time to plan your escape. Surely, he's going to save the kids, so maybe you can crawl through the window above the commode. You get up on the toilet, but you slip on the blood from the dead sex trafficker and fall to the ground. Not the first time today you've fallen like this. You are trying to pull yourself up when you hear the door open. Rome Samuels pushes into the room, moving the body of the dead trafficker out of the way. He lunges for you, tackling you to the floor. The two of you grapple for a moment. First, he has the upper hand, then you, then him again. You're not going to let this guy beat you. There are so many sex traffickers you still need to kill and eat.

He's on top of you when he pulls a machete out of his belt. You try to block the first swing of the blade with your hand, but it lops your hand right off. He raises the machete again. "It wasn't me!" you say, shocked by the clarity of the voice coming out of your mouth. He doesn't heed your warning, swinging the blade at you. You feel your head severed from your body. You don't die immediately from the loss of your head. Your brain is still operating, though you can feel yourself beginning to fade. Your eyes blink slowly as you watch the zombie hunter stand up and walk over to your head, kicking it across the warehouse. The whole world spins around you. Your last thought is "At least I died a hero."

If you have massacred the cultists that resurrected you, go to page 95.

If you have not massacred the cultists that resurrected you, go to page 57.

About the Author

Maxim Volk (they/he) is not in a cult anymore. Now they write things. Horrible things. Terrible things. Things that are sure to make God regret dropping Adam and Eve in that garden with no pants on. Their work has appeared in *Carnage House*, *Macabre Magazine*, and more. They currently live in the US Midwest.

www.ingramcontent.com/pod-product-compliance
Lightning Source LLC
Chambersburg PA
CBHW022217050726
47590CB00002B/841

9781764488426